D1488102

.BRIDGER.

The Story of a Mountain Man

DAVID KHERDIAN

BRIDGER
☐ The Story of a Mountain Man ☐

GREENWILLOW BOOKS, New York

Chief Arapooish's speech appearing in Chapter 5 is from Washington Irving's *The Adventures of Captain Bonneville*, Chapter XXII.

Typeset by Fisher Composition, Inc.
First Edition   1 2 3 4 5 6 7 8 9 10

Library of Congress Cataloging-in-Publication Data
Kherdian, David.
Bridger : the story of a mountain man.
Summary: In 1822 eighteen-year-old Jim Bridger leaves
civilization behind and journeys into the frontier
wilderness, where he learns to trap beaver, experiences
skirmishes with hostile Indians, and explores new country.
1. Bridger, James, 1804–1881—Juvenile fiction.
[1. Bridger, James, 1804–1881—Fiction.
2. Frontier and pioneer life—Fiction.
3. West (U.S.)—Fiction]   I. Title.
PZ7.K527Br 1987   [Fic]   86-7558
ISBN 0-688-06510-4

. TO EDWIN HEDGE .

CONTENTS

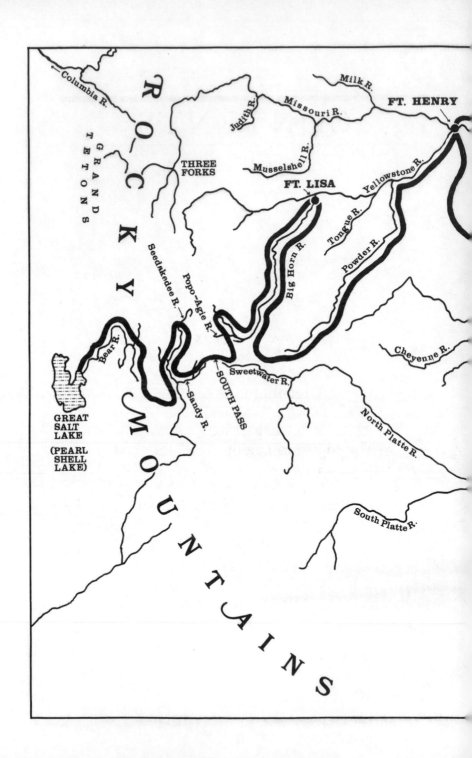

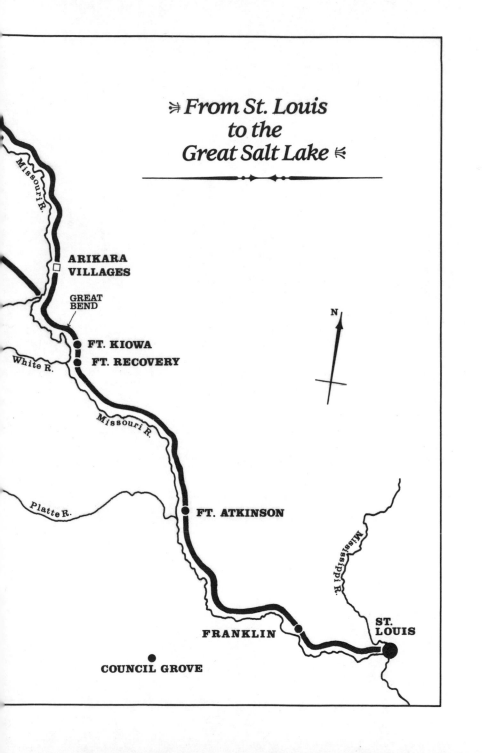

From St. Louis to the Great Salt Lake

Missouri R.

ARIKARA VILLAGES

GREAT BEND

FT. KIOWA

FT. RECOVERY

White R.

Missouri R.

N

Platte R.

FT. ATKINSON

Mississippi R.

FRANKLIN

ST. LOUIS

COUNCIL GROVE

PART ONE

Greenhorn

1822

.1.

"NEXT WEEK!" I COULDN'T STOP saying the words that kept repeating themselves over and over inside my head. It made me feel light-headed, almost as if I couldn't do my job. Who would have thought that two words as simple as these could mean so much. Not "five years," which was how long I'd been bound, not "freedom," which was what I would soon have, but "next week"—because that was when I *would* be free. At last the time was almost here; next week . . .

"Jim, as soon as you get that wagon wheel pinned, I'd like you to take this bay out to the trough for a drink. A walk around the square wouldn't hurt, either. Calm her down a bit. Her owner should be here anytime now to fetch her."

The bay snorted and curled her lips back when I took her by the bridle. "Steady, girl," I said, "there must be a good reason you got new shoes today." She snorted again and looked at me down her long nose. She wasn't taking a talking-to by a young blacksmith. I wondered who her master was. I hadn't seen the man who brought her in.

After she'd had her fill of water I led her around the square, as Mr. Creamer had asked me to. When I got to the billing post, I stopped, as I had so many times before, and stood in front of the notice that by now I had learned by heart.

TO ENTERPRISING YOUNG MEN

The subscriber wishes to engage one hundred men to ascend the river Missouri to its source, there to be employed for one, two or three years—for particulars, enquire of Major Andrew Henry, near the lead mines, in the County of Washington (who will ascend with and command the party), or to the subscriber at St. Louis.

Wm. H. Ashley

"You fixin' to apply?" a voice at my back said. I wheeled around, feeling for some reason that I had been caught out.

"Why so startled?" the voice said.

My mouth was hanging open. The man I was facing was a mountaineer—*a real mountaineer*—dressed in buckskin jacket and leggings and with a sash around his middle that held a knife and pistol. I would never have had the nerve to talk to a mountaineer on my own, and here was one talking to *me*.

A gust of wind blew up. He gave his slouched hat a tug. "Johnson Gardner," he said, putting out his hand. "I've come for my bay." As he spoke, he leaned his head forward, just slightly, and gave me a piercing look. His eyes were gray. He was tall and gaunt, and his skin was tanned a leathery brown. The eagle

4

feather in the band of his hat quivered. "You have a hankering for the mountains?" he asked.

"All my life, Mr. Gardner. I've never dreamed of anything else."

"All your life," he said, smiling. "That can't have been very long. How long you been a bound boy?"

"Five years. That's how long I've been in St. Louis. Before that we lived at Six-Mile Prairie. Before my father died. My mother died before that. I used to trap there, and I hunted some. I own a canoe—"

"Slow down, son. You have any living kin?"

"Just a sister—and an aunt. But I live with Mr. and Mrs. Creamer now."

"For how long are you still bound?" he asked.

"My apprenticeship will be up this week. Do you think General Ashley would take me on, Mr. Gardner?"

"How you gonna know if you don't apply? Let's go see Phil Creamer. I need to settle up."

We walked back to the blacksmith shop without talking. I still had hold of the bay, but she kept pulling at the reins and nudging her master on the forearm with her nose.

"Hello, Johnson," Mr. Creamer said when we entered the shop. "That's a fine horse you've got there. Got her shoed and ready. Where you headed for now?"

"I've signed on with Ashley."

"I knew it!" Mr. Creamer exclaimed. "I just knew it! Didn't you serve with Major Henry on the Big Horn a few years back?"

"You've got a good memory, Phil. But this time I aim to trap. We killed more Blackfeet than beaver that trip."

"Missouri's opened up some, I'd say," Phil Creamer answered. "All those military forts. Pelts are bringing good money for the man willing to go after them."

Johnson Gardner turned and looked me in the eye. "You want to go to the mountains, then you'll have to pay—you'll have to pay every mile of the way. There's starvin' times and grizzlies—"

"I've heard tell," I answered. My knees were shaking, but I held my ground. "I know what's called for and I know the price—but I aim to be a free man, and I want to choose how I'll be free. Out there a man can dress to suit himself, and go where he pleases, and be a part of something, come what may. Except for my kin, I ain't leaving nothing behind but my bondage—"

Mr. Creamer was about to say something. I knew I'd spoken out of turn, but my chance had come and I had to take it. Johnson Gardner held his hand up to Mr. Creamer to silence him. Then he spoke. "I'll see what I can do," he said, his face expressionless. "Hang up your apron and come with me. I'll be moseying down to the river, past General Ashley's office."

He turned to Mr. Creamer for permission, but Mr.

Creamer had turned away, shrugging his shoulders. "All right," he said at last. "All right, go!"

"I'll make up the time," I called after Mr. Creamer. "I won't leave beholdin'."

The hiring hall was in a storefront building that appeared to be empty from the outside. I handed the reins to Johnson Gardner and watched him mount his bay. He had his face turned toward the Mississippi. My eyes followed his gaze beyond the trees, over the water, as far as the eye could see.

I was standing in the doorway that Johnson Gardner had motioned me to a moment before. "In there," he had said, indicating the door with his raised arm.

They don't say good-bye in the mountains, I thought. Or hello. They say how, same as the Indians do. I knew because I had heard them from a distance, greeting each other in the streets.

General Ashley was seated with an assistant at two long tables placed end to end to serve as a reviewing desk. I had moved forward in line to his assistant's command of "Next!"

This time the voice belonged to General Ashley. "Your name?"

"Bridger, sir—James Bridger."

"Date of birth?"

"March 17, 1804."

"That makes you eighteen—as of last week." General Ashley raised his eyebrows and stared at me. I noted that his eyes were the same gray-blue as mine. I knew what he was thinking, so I spoke before he could ask me another question. "I'm not too young for the work, sir. I've trapped beaver and otter and muskrat. I own my own gun and canoe—"

"How about your parents?"

"I've been orphaned—my aunt and sister are moving back to Richmond—"

"You Virginia-born?"

"Yes, sir. We moved away when I was a youngster. We've been living here and nearabouts since 1812."

"Education?"

"I've been schooled some at home."

"Skills?"

"Blacksmithing, sir. I've completed my apprenticeship. I've been bound to Phil Creamer since I was thirteen."

I didn't see how blacksmithing could come in handy in a beaver stream, but I could tell by General Ashley's smile that he was pleased. There was probably a whole lot to trapping beaver that I didn't know anything about. General Ashley continued to study me from under his eyebrows. He was rolling a pencil between his hands. I could see he was thinking.

"Sir, I want to work and I want to learn. I want to go to the mountains—"

"I wasn't planning on taking anyone under twenty,

but you've been doing man's work for five years, and it isn't likely you'll get homesick halfway up the Missouri."

He turned and spoke to his assistant. "He's got some filling out to do, but he's got a frame that will accommodate growing. Mark him for the first keelboat."

General Ashley turned to me again. "You'll be setting out the third of April, under charge of Major Andrew Henry."

My face must have been beaming. "You know of Major Henry, then?" the general asked.

"Of course, sir."

"And Mike Fink and his sidekicks, Carpenter and Talbot?"

I didn't know what to say. There wasn't anything *to* say. These names belonged to legend. Although I knew these men existed, I never dreamed that I would one day make their acquaintance, let alone work in their company.

"Take my advice and study Mike Fink, but from a distance. All the keelers and mountain men are loners, but if they take a liking to you . . . well, everyone likes to tell what they know. Ask questions and study their ways. You can stow your canoe with us. Bring your gun and your possibles on the third. Early! That's next Wednesday. We'll be pushing off first thing, to make the Missouri by nightfall."

.2.

Wednesday finally arrived. Our keelboat was docked just beyond Ashley's headquarters. It was still too dark to see that far upriver when I turned the corner onto the street I had last walked with Johnson Gardner. A cow was lowing in the distance, perhaps in answer to the keelboat's horn, that sounded through the morning mist shrouding the dark brown waters of the Mississippi.

It wasn't long before the keelboat hove into sight. I hurried to the shore, my heart pounding under my hickory shirt, my rigging and gun suddenly as light as goose-down packing. Men were moving about, taking instructions from a man I was sure was Mike Fink. I didn't notice the fiddler until I heard him. He was seated atop the cabin, fiddling a tune as sweet as the purr of a cat.

Someone had fallen into step beside me. I felt his feet moving along on the hard ground before I turned to have a look at his face.

He smiled when our eyes met. "Hello, greenhorn," he said. "I reckon we're headed for the same place." He was of medium height, with sorrel hair and a stubby, brownish beard. There was a straw dangling from his mouth. I took him to be in his early twenties. "Up the Big Muddy," I said, returning the smile.

"'To its source, there to be employed for one, two, or three years.' Don't look so serious, you can always jump a flatboat coming the other way, if it gets to be too disagreeable."

"I'm signed up," I answered, "for whatever's in store."

"Running away from something?"

"No, towards something."

His smile caused two brown spots to form on his cheeks, that quickly turned back to freckles when he spoke again. "Name's Daniel T. Potts. Some call me Dan, most call me Potts."

"Jim Bridger," I said.

"Shake hands, friend."

The men had formed a double line below the plank. As they boarded, they were yanked aboard by the *voyageurs*, whom we had no trouble distinguishing because of their bright red shirts and red woolen sashes. They were laughing and joking in French, and I understood at once that this was their way of greeting the mountaineers. Theirs was the job of getting us upriver. The country beyond might belong to us, but the boat that was to take us there and return with our cache belonged to them.

"This is my first keelboat," I said to Potts as we were being yanked aboard. "Biggest boat I've been on before is my canoe, that I used to paddle to St. Louis when I lived in Six-Mile Prairie."

Potts laughed. "You gonna miss her?"

"Probably not," I answered. "She's here somewhere. I managed to get her down here last Sunday for loading."

"Anyone seeing you off?"

"No," I answered, "and yourself?"

"Family's back East," Potts replied.

We were all loaded now, each of us scrambling about as best we could to make a place for ourselves. I took the boat to be about seventy feet long. There was some room along the *passe avant*, but it was taken up by the *voyageurs*, who were leaning against their poles and singing to themselves in French. They were obviously pleased to be on the water.

Not so the fiddler, who was in no mood to play with so many people suddenly crowding around him. His frown was in sharp contrast to the cheery mood with which he had greeted the newcomers aboard, fiddling a tune he seemed to be composing on the spot.

I don't know how many cats there were aboard, but the two I saw, a black and a tawny, were skulking about.

"Why do we have cats aboard?" I asked.

"Wait till we hit the Missouri," a voice at my side said. "Beats me, but whenever the boat docks, the mice come on. In the night. Everyone likes free doin's, even mice. If it weren't for these cats, we'd lose our provisions in a week."

At that moment the swivel fired, followed by a shout from the shore, and the shooting off of rifles in the crowd. I looked out at the smiling faces and waving arms, and all at once I recognized two faces in the middle of the crowd: Auntie and my sister. I lifted my arms and shouted. They threw their arms up at once, but I could tell they had been crying. I had told them not to see me off. I had thought I couldn't bear the parting, but this was even worse. Auntie had her hankie out, and between waves she was daubing at her eyes. They were holding hands, and my sister waved at me feebly, trying not to show she, too, was crying.

The boat was moving fast. "Good-bye!" I shouted. "Good-bye, good-bye!" But I knew they couldn't hear me.

I stayed on the deck, waving, until they were long out of sight.

.3.

Our sails were up now, a steady wind at our stern. On the western bank our herd of fifty horses moved in sight of the boat.

"We'll be needing those horses when we get to the

Yellowstone," I said to Potts. We were sitting shoulder-to-shoulder against the cargo box, facing the sweeps.

"You're mighty noticin'," Potts said. "I get the notion there's more going on inside your head than you allow."

"I'm not a clever talker, if that's what you mean."

"Maybe not. But it don't hurt none to try. You're gonna be up against some fancy yarn spinners. I'm told these old coons go at tall-tale telling like it was part of the trade. Maybe it is. There's more to this life than mountains and meadows and beaver to trap, I fancy."

"That's Johnson Gardner riding lead," I said, pointing across river. "I met him last week. We shoed his mount, that's how I know those horses are ours. I'm hoping he'll take me under his wing, teach me the ropes."

"What you fixin' to learn? I mean, that you reckon will help you become a mountain man?"

"I don't know. That's a good question. Like you say, there's more to it than trapping beaver. We'll have to learn Injun ways, when the time comes. But right now I'm thinking I'd like to learn the French language."

"Now what made you come up with a notion like that?"

"Just the feeling these *voyageurs* have about song.

And that fiddler up there, his fiddlin' is *beaucoup* French."

Potts laughed. "If you ain't half horse and half alligator, I don't know what. Didn't you tell me that you never learned your letters proper, and now you're pining to learn French?"

"Aren't the French big in the trade? And the Spanish, too? A westering man ought to know it all—Injun, Spanish, French. Sign language, too, and all the rest of it."

The wind had shifted while we talked, moving from south to east, and then slowly subsiding, calming the river and raising the sound of our voices.

"The *voyageurs* have moved to the oars," Potts said, changing the subject. "But six pairs at the sweeps won't do much with this cargo of men and goods."

"It's certain sure they can't pole in this water," I said. "Too deep. At least we made good time while we had the wind at our backs. I hope we make the Big Muddy by nightfall."

Potts turned and looked over the water we had traveled. St. Louis had disappeared but for a high bluff of land that was still visible. "Nobody's saying much about it," Potts said, "but this here party, and Ashley's boat, is going to change the fur trade—if it all works out."

"Don't rightly follow you," I said.

"I mean, we're not going to be wagers. We're going to be paid for what we bring in. You trap good, you get paid good. And Ashley and Henry are putting up gun, powder, and the rest. It's a step up for the trapper, that's certain."

As he spoke, Potts got to his feet and began stretching his legs. I let my attention float out over the water, picking up the riders in the herd. Johnson Gardner was riding lead, all right, his hair flowing from under his broad-brimmed hat. What Potts had said was true. It put me to thinking what it would be like if there were free trappers who went wherever they liked and sold to whomever they could. Hudson's Bay and the rest of the companies didn't own the streams—and the Indians only thought they did. But the outfits did have the forts, and without the forts you couldn't sell. Without the forts and trading posts you couldn't do anything.

The men were heaving at the sweeps now, their fellow *voyageurs* encouraging them on with song. Even the fiddler had taken up his bow and had joined in for the race up the river. Although I couldn't see it, I was pretty sure the Missouri would be coming up soon.

At last it appeared, and when it did the men began shouting and waving their caps, as if they were calling to a friend. Mike Fink's voice rose above the rest. "There you are, you heartless whore of a river," he roared. "It may take us the summer to go all the way up ye, but we'll never turn back, that's sure!"

It was an awesome sight, its brown waters charging into the Mississippi as if they had crashed through a dike. Broken and uprooted trees were being hurled over the surface, while in the backwater opposite we could see the bloated back of a huge animal, either buffalo or bear.

"God a'mighty," Potts said, half under his breath, "the only thing qualified to navigate that river is bird."

I was too overcome to speak. Out of the corner of my eye I caught sight of a gray beard and looked up to see a buffalo-coated man who was obviously a veteran trapper. He was using his gun for ballast. He turned and looked at me from around his gun, that was nearly as tall as he was. He was smiling, a smile that could have meant most anything. "We'll clumb that two-tit wonder," he said. "We'll clumb her on the backs of these Creoles, and we won't leave off sweating till we do. You make this river once, you'll never fear cold or starvation again. *If'n* you make her. Some do, some don't; which side of the fence you greenhorns gonna land on, I wonder."

We were all standing now, the wind at our stern, pushing us across the lapping waters of the Mississippi.

"Some call it 'Swimming Timber,'" another man said.

"And some call it worse," the graybeard answered.

"We've got the wind," the other said. "Without

17

that wind we'd have no chance. We'll slide in under that cutbank. You'll see. Just watch Fink, this is where that cussed steersman shines."

Five ravens were batting their wings, held stationary by the wind. I wondered if I would ever be heading back as they were, or if the wind that was blowing us in was a good omen.

The ravens cawed now, straight overhead, and darted downriver on set wings, as if they had been released from an airborne cage.

The wind had pushed us in. Hugging the bank, we sailed toward a sun that appeared to be setting among a furrow of windy trees, but that was as far away as a dream.

.4.

A horse whinnying somewhere on the opposite shore wakened me from a deep sleep. I turned over in the half dark and stared into the coals of last night's fire. It was only then that I realized that the horses were ours and that their riders must also be awake.

"You look fer it to warm, when it does we'll get the rains." The speaker was Moses "Black" Harris, the graybeard that had first spoken to me on the boat. We were standing on the bank, watching the keelboat move upriver. "Most of you will hunt along the bank," Harris went on, "in case you're needed for cordeling, to help out the *voyageurs*. You know what cordeling is?"

There was a crowd of us now on the bank, watching the boat and listening to Harris, who was obviously in charge of the land party.

"That means you pull that cussed boat with a rope—from the bank, or waist-deep in the water— whatever it takes to get her up that river."

"Wind feels right for the sails," someone declared.

"River changes course too fast," Harris said, "and even then you don't want to get your charge up and jam up against an *embarrass*."

"What's that?" Potts asked.

"Island of debris collecting around a squall." Harris pointed ahead. "That's what you get every time the channel changes—and sometimes when it doesn't."

"This must be a channel-changing river," I said. From where we stood the river was dotted with *embarrass*.

"Looks like we're in for a real climb," Potts whispered at my side. "You know, Jim, I was thinking last night before I fell asleep that life has given you a hard go—taking your mammy and pappy away and all, and I know how you feel being out of bondage and free, with the mountains calling—and I feel it all the same as you, but it's only true for me when I look up the river toward that dream we're heading for—"

"What you trying to tell me, Potts?" I broke in.

"Just that when I look down the river, I remember my family in the East, successful business folk wanting me to join in and take my rightful place. But it's not for me. I want to be an adventurer and a trapper, same as you."

"You got a point," I said. "I never looked at it that way, but a man with no choice is sometimes better off than one who is being pulled two ways at once. But I worry about my sister, I do. I know my aunt'll care for her, but I aim to send her some money for schooling. A man like me can get by without schooling, but if she's going to be a lady, she'll need educating."

We were walking into a clearing, and I watched as Harris moved off by himself and stood at its edge. He was calling turkey, his body poised, his rifle aimed at the ready. All at once he fired and ran into a partial thicket where we could hear the turkey he had shot thrashing about.

"Tomorrow will be better," Harris said while tying the turkey to his belt. "If we can move the boat to the other shore, we can ride out for bigger game. Every year the game gets pushed back a little further."

The horn had sounded while Harris spoke. "That's for us," one of the men said. "Let's head back."

We could hear Mike Fink cursing before we caught sight of the boat, so we knew something was wrong. "As long as a man's cursing," Potts said over his shoulder, "you can be sure it's none too bad." I knew what Potts meant, especially as it applied to a man like Fink.

The keelboat had gotten itself beached on a sandbar. "She's headed upriver, at least," Harris said. We were standing on the bank, watching the men on the rope, the water nearly to their chests. "They must have been cordeling," Harris went on, "or she wouldn't be where she is now. Once that current moves a keeler sidewise, she's a goner. That river'll turn her over and smash her in two faster than it takes to say so."

"Let's go, you men," Major Henry shouted to us from atop the cargo box. "Everyone to the boat."

We jumped into the icy water and fought our way through the swirling current to the bow of the boat.

"Throw your guns and rigging aboard and help with the rope." Major Henry turned his attention to the men tugging at the other end. "Work her easy," he shouted. "We gotta bring her out of here slow enough to guide her."

Other men were wading toward the boat now. Mike Fink was kneeling on the floor beside the man who had spelled him on the rudder. No one else, other than Major Henry, was on board. "Some of you help keep the driftwood off the bow. The boat's got to be clear or she won't drift free. Once we get her loose—" Major Henry's voice was momentarily lost in the roar of the river and the cursing men.

He must have spotted more men on shore because his voice suddenly bellowed over my head. "You two—run out to the point ahead and keep those drifting logs out of our way."

"Steady, steady . . . I can hear her scraping under me . . . keep her tight now, keep her tight—"

I was fighting my way upstream as fast as I could. There was no one between the men on the rope and the men on the point, who had entered the water now and were struggling together to keep a twisting tree trunk from entering the channel created by the shoal.

Suddenly the log sprang free, twirled around in the current, and came charging down toward the keelboat. I had to divert that log before it banged our boat and knocked it off the sandbar. I swam quickly to the end closest to me and began pushing it, but the current was too strong. I swam to the other side of the log and pushed, but I couldn't make it budge. I twisted my body onto the log and scissored my legs around it, and at that moment it lurched and I felt my left ankle get caught on one of the broken branches. I couldn't get it free, nor could I get the log to turn so my body would be above water. My face and arms were bruised in the effort to keep myself from drowning. I knew the log was heading for the boat, and any second we would crash into its side and I would be crushed. I felt a sudden *whoosh*, and struggling upward, I could make out Potts's freckled face at the end of the log. The next thing I saw was a face overhead, as the log brushed the side of the boat, then whirled about, freeing my leg as it swung out of the current into still water. Without thinking I floated downriver, stunned, confused, but very much alive.

When I scrambled onto the bank and looked upriver, the keelboat was free and being pulled toward shore. Potts had saved my life.

.5.

That evening we were given our first taste of liquor.

I took a cup and let it be filled when my turn came. Potts looked at me and smiled. "You'll get on," he said. "It's hard to figure how something tasting so awful the first time can come to mean so much to a man as time goes on."

"I thought liquor was prohibited in the trade—except for the *voyageurs*," I said.

Gardner was sitting nearby, listening to our conversation. "That's so," he said, and took a sip from his cup. "But the patroons carry a lot of liquor. There isn't much law to keep to west of the Mississippi."

"We'll get a taste now and then," Gardner continued. "At least till we get above the forts. Not many'll turn back above the Platte." He looked over at Harris for confirmation.

The first sip burned my throat, but though I avoided coughing, it made my eyes smart and water.

"It's been diluted," Potts said, "but it ain't half bad."

I took another sip from my cup and sat back to have a look at the other men. The *voyageurs* had left their campsite to drink with us. Everyone seemed to be talking at once, in contrast to the night before, when the men spoke in whispers or not at all, as if they were preparing in advance for the caution that would be required once we reached Indian country. But all that was forgotten now.

Mike Fink's voice rose above the rest. He was singing in French, his voice distinguishable from the voices of the Creoles because of its volume and accent.

"This is his first trip up the Missouri," Gardner said. "The brothels and grogshops are pretty scarce once you leave the Mississippi. He's gonna have a hard time of it, les'n he takes a shine to trapping and mountain life."

"Why did he leave the Big River?" Potts asked.

"Steamboats are coming. Keelboats won't be plying the Mississippi much longer, I reckon. Mike wanted to make the jump before he was forced to it."

Fink finished his song and went into a jig. When he was done, he looked around the fire at us and over at the Creoles, who had drifted away and were sitting in a group by themselves. But at Fink's command—"The cups, Carpenter, me boy, let's show the boys the cups"—they stirred to their feet and edged closer to where the rest of us were seated. "Let's show them how a keelboatman can handle a rifle."

Young Carpenter assented with a nod, and Talbot flipped a coin.

"Yours is the first shot, hoss," Mike bellowed, and placing his cup steadily on his head, he waited, flintlock at his side.

Carpenter paced off seventy yards, counting as he walked, his rifle in one hand, his cup in the other. When he turned, he slowly bent down and placed his cup on the ground. Then he took steady aim and fired. The cup flew from Fink's head, spilling whiskey in a spray.

The Creoles cheered.

Now it was Fink's turn.

Behind Carpenter's head the horizon glowed orange. Far away, tiny birds, the size of leaves, moved as a wave, unhurried and silent.

It hardly seemed that Fink aimed. The cup flew from Carpenter's head an instant before the volley sounded. The men ran to meet each other and embraced, Mike Fink swinging Carpenter in the air in a bear hug. The Creoles crowded around them, slapping their backs, while the men by the fire continued sipping their whiskey as if nothing had happened.

As best I could tell, the look on Major Henry's face was one of amused silence. Gardner's face was expressionless.

I sat, sipping my whiskey with the others, but with one new thought after another going on inside my head. After a time I moved off by myself and lay under a tree. The moon was traveling upward, slicing through the spindly branches of cottonwood. As it moved, it seemed to be pouring its full light onto the boat. There was something in the silence that made it all seem mysterious. Our boisterousness, our worries and triumphs seemed to belong to another world. I watched the moon climb to its height through the streaking clouds as thin as silk ribbons. Slowly I closed my eyes and fell asleep.

.6.

I awoke to the sound of busy feet moving over the rushes that had been stamped down the night before when we made our camp. The cook was stirring the pot that hung over the fire. Gardner sat nearby, filling his pipe, his buckskins glistening in the half-light. He reached a twig over to the fire and lit his pipe. I wondered why he had been staring at me.

From somewhere behind me I heard Major Henry speak. "No more whiskey till we get beyond the settlements."

"It was a mistake," the other voice said.

"Not till we get beyond Franklin," Major Henry continued. "He must have taken the boy's canoe."

"Bridger's?"

"Yes, Bridger's."

"Don't worry, he'll be back, and Carpenter with him."

"See that everyone's fed and ready by sunup," Major Henry ordered. "They'll either catch up or get left behind."

No one spoke as we ate. Major Henry was poking with one hand at the fire, a tin of coffee in the other hand.

"Work and whiskey don't mix," Harris said, turning his head in Major Henry's direction.

Major Henry looked from one man to another. "We've got beaver to trap and buffalo to hunt—not to mention goats and deer and sheep. And fighting grizzlies, and maybe Injuns. These boatmen would rather run naked across the prairie than face an angry Injun. The closer you get to the mountains, the happier you feel inside. Admit it! But the farther they get from the Mississippi, the more morose they become. Only whiskey can cheer them then. That and women. Hell, you'd rather wrestle a grizzly than do what they do. But think of it! There'd be no expedition without them. Anyone can take a cache of furs downstream, but only these *voyageurs* can take the trapper up this impossible river."

Gardner adjusted his powder horn and looked off toward the boat. Harris followed his gaze.

"I want you men to stay out of the cottonwood thickets," Major Henry said. He was staring, first at Harris, then at Gardner. "This is grizzly country. I can afford to lose Fink, I can't afford to lose you two."

"Every year the game gets pushed further back," Harris said. "I'll get something bigger than turkey and squirrel today or else—"

"Stay close at hand—all of you," Major Henry commanded. "We've got plenty of food—for now. What we need is to get upriver in time for the fall hunt."

.7.

Harris and I were wading along the shore. The keelboat had crossed the current to the other bank, where it was being cordeled. Although we couldn't wade out far enough to escape the swarms of mosquitoes, we were at least free of the wood ticks. The bank was a tangle of brush and wild grapevines, and wherever fallen trees had snagged against the bank, nettles grew the size of a man.

"I've never seen yellow-gray water before," I said to Harris. We had hold of a tree stump that we were trying to coax into the current.

"This is the Missouri at its worst. The further we get from civilization, the better I like it, and the better the river likes it, too. Down here it's the color of disease—but you'll see, it changes as we go. It'll be brown before it's green, but it'll be blue when we come to its source. That's when this child will be happy."

We watched a pirogue round the bend, riding low in the water, one man paddling, another sitting half propped against a bundle in the middle of the boat, his rifle close at hand. A coal-black cat on a leash sat facing our direction, its eyes reflecting the color of the water as the boat drew near.

Harris and the men in the boat seemed to recognize one another. "Is that you, old hoss?" the man at the stern called out, raising his paddle overhead in salute.

Harris gave a snort, then hollered, "You coons are headin' the wrong way. Beaver's upstream, not down. Wagh! If you ain't a sight for sore eyes."

"We're headed for Red Head's town," the man leaning against the bundle said. The pirogue had reached us now, and we took hold of its side and held it steady in the water. "We're in need of whiskey, hoss, and bacca. Been making cold camp and paddlin' after dark till night before last, when we come to Franklin."

"Say, Harris," the other man asked, "how much they offerin' for pelts in St. Louis?"

"Six dollars a plew for prime. That's spring beaver. But if that there is fall cache, I reckon it won't bring nearly as much. Who ye carryin' for?"

"Josh Pilcher, but we've signed off. Doggone those Blackfoot diggin's," the man at the paddle said, slapping his thigh with his free hand.

"Too many good men went under this spring for us to lose our topknots," the other said.

"Well, I reckon you can handle the Injuns in St. Louis, all right," Harris said. "Foofaraw and firewater's all they need. There won't be any more bufler for them, or you neither, looks like."

The second man looked at Harris and then upriver. "This coon ain't done with those mountains, not by a long chalk. You must be with Major Henry's band." He turned his gaze toward me for the first time. "Josh Pilcher read us Hempstead's letter written from St. Louis about the time you signed on. You must have cleaned out the grogshops putting together upwards of one hundred men. Is this one of the greenhorns?" he went on, pointing his paddle in my direction.

I looked over at the cat, who was either looking at me or at nothing.

"He don't know to keep his powder dry," Harris was saying, "but General Ashley's taken a shine to him. He's got the makings, I reckon, if he can keep his hair long enough to learn Injun ways and trappers' ways both."

"Seems to me Hempstead said yours was the first boat. Is General Ashley bringing the second boat up himself?"

"Can't say. Only know she's been called the *Enterprize*. You figure to join up?"

"We're not figuring our next move yet. We'll see what happens after we unload these plews. Say, you wouldn't have any bacca—this beaver feels like a chaw."

Harris broke off two pieces from his plug and handed it down. The men took it in turn, nodding their heads in thanks. Without another word the boat began to drift free.

"You take the bark off those Blackfeet," the man at the stern said. "We'll be back sure, you hear!"

"You ain't seen Fink?" Harris called after them.

Instead of answering the man pointed. We turned to see two men in a canoe turning a bend in the river.

It was my canoe. I recognized it before I did the men.

.8.

I'd been thinking about what Harris had said to those veteran trappers in the pirogue—that I didn't know to keep my powder dry. It took me awhile to connect it to the looks he and Gardner had given me one morning. I remembered now waking and looking up to see Harris casting a cold eye at me from over by the camp fire.

But this was only half of it. The important thing he let slip was that General Ashley had taken a shine to me. If Ashley saw that I had the makings of a trapper it was likely that he would ask a veteran like Harris to look after me and train me—if he could.

I began observing Harris as he bedded down. I could see that there was a method to the way he made camp for the night. Even though we weren't in Indian territory, it was plain that he never relaxed his guard. I knew this about him—and Gardner, too—they were ever on the alert and ready for anything that might come along. They slept with their guns and powder horns within quick reach, so they could grab them both in one easy motion the minute they woke up. Indians, and especially the Blackfeet, were famous for sneaking into a white man's camp in the dead of night to steal horses.

I was also learning to listen, to study the patterns and habits of animals, and to use my eyes in every way I could.

One day Harris said to me, "You seem to go in for lots of backwards and forwards studying. Just what is it you're studying on?"

"I don't know how to say it in words," I answered.

"I want to learn all about the land. What it looks like from any direction. Coming back down this river, it ain't gonna look the way it did going upriver, and if you come towards this spot from the east, it looks different than coming to it from the west. If I just see it from one direction, it don't register, but if I can see it from all four directions at once, it's like a picture that moves. It stays in my head."

"If that don't beat all," Harris said, slapping his knee. "Sounds like you've got a map inside your head and you add bits as we go along."

"That's it!" I exclaimed, growing excited. "A continuing picture. I've got the whole trip so far 'mapped' inside my head."

"That's a gift, Jim Bridger, don't ever think it ain't. You're gonna have something inside you prettier than poetry before you're done."

.9.

It must have been the end of April when we reached Franklin, the last settlement of any size on our way up the Missouri. The men were excited for reasons I couldn't quite fathom.

Major Henry gave leave to all but a small guard to go ashore for one hour. I chose to stay on board. There was something peaceful in being alone—or nearly alone—aboard our usually crowded boat. I sat propped against the mast, the town of Franklin on my left and the vast wilderness in every other direction. The ducks were still flying in numbers, and high above them a formation of swans could be seen. The flow of ice in the river had stopped, and the weather was beginning to warm. This was the first day in three that it hadn't rained. We expected to make good time from here on out.

Potts came back aboard ahead of everyone else. He was carrying a newspaper under his arm. He smelled faintly of whiskey. "I had one with the boys," he said, "but it didn't interest me none to be with those greenhorns, so I bought the *Intelligencer* and here I am."

"What's the *Intelligencer*?" I asked.

"The local paper, as you can see. I was hoping there would be news of Ashley, and there is. They've set off on the *Enterprize*, and they've got some veterans aboard, they have. Thomas Eddie for one, and a young bible-toter by the name of Jedediah Smith. Ashley's stayed behind, though. Daniel Moore's at the helm. Never heard of him, have you?"

Major Henry had come aboard and was walking along the *passe avant*. When he stood beneath us, he stopped and called up, "How would you boys like to get us some catfish?"

"Catfish, sir?" Potts queried.

"There's a feeder stream upriver a couple of miles that's choked with fish. Catfish up to fifty pounds, I'm told. One of you paddle, the other spear. We need a change from squirrel and turkey."

Potts and I jumped up at once. This was more to our liking than sitting around and waiting for good and bad fortune to take their turns.

"We'll be upriver," Major Henry said. "Fish as long as you like, but make sure to get back in time to shove off."

"This is a sight better than any duty we've been given till now," Potts said as we paddled across river in my canoe.

It wasn't long before the feeder stream came into view. It was only about twenty feet across at the mouth. We had no more than turned into it than the roar of the Missouri began to subside. The sheltered quiet of the stream—that looked like it had never been traveled before—made me realize that I had long ago ceased to hear the sound of the Missouri.

It took my eyes a time to get accustomed to the stream's bottom. The catfish were there, all right, but so big that they seemed to *be* the bottom and not just on it. They lay in the sludge, brown as mud and lazy as stone. Only their whiskers finally gave them away. It wasn't two hours before we had four fish, all our canoe would safely hold. I got to spear the last fish, which turned out to be the biggest one of all. "Must be a thirty-pounder," I said, beaming, holding it up for Potts to see.

"I've never seen you so cheerful," Potts said. "If'n you swell up any more, you'll burst your britches."

"It ain't pride," I said, "just fun. This is the first fishing I've done that I can remember."

Potts looked at me seriously and then smiled. "I guess you were pretty busy looking after things when your daddy died."

"I guess so."

"I'm glad we had the chance for a little fun."

"I'm glad, too." I put down my catfish and took the paddle from Potts. I wanted to have something for my hands to do and to feel the wind in my face. I was feeling good inside and happy about the catfish we had caught.

Potts gave a whoop as we swept back into the Missouri. "Wait till the boys see these!" he shouted into its welcoming roar.

.10.

By July the rains had ended and the weather had warmed up, changing the river's color and disposition. We were in sight of our next destination: the Platte River, the symbolic halfway point of our journey.

It must have been near noon when we reached it, a favoring breeze at our stern, with our square sail full-set. Off in the distance the green hills, round and treeless, reminded me how much the terrain had changed since we had embarked on our journey.

Surely we would be coming to buffalo country soon. We had seen our share of deer and wild pig and had been lucky enough to shoot a deer. Our diet had improved with the country, which was becoming wild, broad, and promising.

In the morning all hands boarded ship so we could mark the occasion as a body. From the glints in the eyes of the veterans I should have guessed there was another reason as well. I realized it when I saw that all of us greenhorns were at the bow of the boat, while the rest of the men were at the stern. How this had happened without my noticing it, I don't know, but it suddenly hit me. I looked over at Potts, who nodded knowingly but said nothing. As I glanced about at all the young faces, I spotted Major Henry standing atop the cargo box.

In a laughing voice he announced, "Boys, we are about to make men of ye. Whether we will succeed or not remains to be seen, but today we are going to wash off some of that green . . . and maybe lift a little hair."

I didn't know at first what he meant, but I began to have an idea when I noticed that Mike Fink and Carpenter, who were seated at Major Henry's side, were strapping their razors.

"Fiddler, what say ye?" Major Henry commanded. The fiddler, seated atop his special box, began to play a tune that I could swear seemed to be rising and falling before ending in a splash.

And that was how it happened.

We were hurled overboard, first by ones and twos, and then by threes and fours, until we decided it was useless to struggle and began plunging overboard on our own.

Less green or not, I hoisted myself back on board, cold and shivering and grateful for the sun that was positioned, for the moment, between two dark clouds.

"Now the real fun begins," Potts said at my side, pointing to a lad who was being wrestled to his knees in front of Fink.

"What will it be?" Major Henry roared down at us wet and shivering rats. "Drinks for your betters or a lesson in shaving? Mike Fink favors the look of the buzzard, and Carpenter, the head of the Pawnee. I can't say for sure which one you'll come out to be."

"I ain't drawed wages," the broken voice of the lad said. Fink had the greenhorn's topknot in one hand, with his poised razor in the other, just an inch or two from its target. The words were hardly out of the young man's mouth when his head began to change from a mop of curly brown into a white, oval egg.

"Lordy," Potts murmured, "that ain't gonna happen to me." He reached inside his leggings and pulled out a coin, flashing it overhead so there would be no mistaking his intentions.

"How about it, Jim," he said, smiling now and feeling safe, "you gonna keep your hair?"

"I reckon hair grows as easily as it comes off—this side of the Platte," I said.

"Don't buffalo me, Jim Bridger. Don't tell me you won't trade a *dinero* to keep from looking like that buzzard over there."

I looked up to see not one buzzard but a whole row of them seated on the cargo box, sliding their hands over their bald pates, as if they refused to believe what they could not see.

The one under Carpenter's hand was going to be a Pawnee, sure enough. There was a string of hair, looking like a patch of bruised grass, atop his skull, while the side of his head was being shaved clean.

"Ain't it comical?" Potts said.

"Depends which side of the fence you're doin' your viewing from," I answered. "I spent my last *dinero* on some foofaraws and vermilion to use in trading."

"Here," Potts said, thrusting a coin in my hand. "A dunking don't deserve to be followed by a shaving, we'll have loads of money soon enough, partner."

. 11 .

We were a crew now, a body, a brigade.

We were also individuals—by force of initiation and through our own identification as "Ashley's Men." We had a place in the fur trade. It would be up to each of us, as men and as a company, to make our mission a success.

Our square sail was up, the river free for the moment of logs and debris, as it spread in a wide green passage to the north.

Everyone had turned their attention to a bluff we were passing. "There she be!" Harris exclaimed, "Council Grove, named by Lewis and Clark after they powwowed with the Injuns."

As Harris spoke, the stars and stripes of Fort Atkinson came into view, followed by its twin towers and whitewashed walls. "This is the last military garrison and the limit of government protection," Major Henry announced.

"It's also the land of the Sioux," Gardner put in.

We docked our boat and walked ashore, the great doors of the fort opening for us. The soldiers cheered as we filed in. We were as anxious for news of the States as they were for news of the happenings up and down the Missouri.

Major Henry was hurriedly called into the office of Colonel Leavenworth, the commander of the fort, while the rest of us gathered around a red-faced sergeant who gave us the news.

Some weeks before—the sergeant wasn't sure just when—Ashley's second boat, the *Enterprize*, had gone under. He didn't have the complete details, but they did know that the *Enterprize*, in turning to avoid a sawyer, had yawed, causing the top of the mast to catch in an overhanging tree. Wheeling out of control, the boat had turned broadside to the current and was swept under in a matter of seconds. All of the men had been saved, but virtually the entire cargo was lost.

"We learned about it just yesterday," the sergeant was saying. "They say Ashley went into action the minute he got news of the disaster. He has another boat and has assembled forty-six recruits. They're already on their way."

"We can trust they'll make good time now," Gardner said. "They'll have to push hard and they will."

We began making bets as to who would command the boat and how soon it would arrive.

"We're having a special mess for you boys," the sergeant bellowed. "Vegetables—and bufler hump."

"Vegetables!" The word chorused among us in disbelief. We hadn't had fresh vegetables to eat since leaving St. Louis.

41

The sergeant waited for our voices to subside before he spoke again. "As soon as your meat bags are full, we're going to set up store, for those of you who have goods to trade."

As we sat down at the long table to eat with the others, I said to Potts, "I'm not going to have any trouble knowing what to trade for."

"What's that?" Potts asked, without letting his eyes stray from the steaming carrots that were headed our way.

"You notice how different the Injuns look here?" I asked. The Indians were the first thing I noticed when we came into the fort. I had seen plenty of soldiers around St. Louis, and all of them looked like the soldiers here—more or less—but the Indians up here in their own country were different from the hang-around-the-fort Indians of St. Louis.

Potts served himself some carrots and passed the bowl to me. "Go on," he said.

"Well, the Injuns look like Injuns, and the soldiers look like soldiers, but we just look like misfits from the settlements. Gardner and Harris and some of the others—they look like something definite, but the rest of us—"

"With trappers it's up to each man to decide for himself. There ain't no rules. Just what's practical."

"I'm trading for moccasins," I said, "and buckskin leggings and a jacket."

"Best concentrate on the food before it's gone," Potts said. "Here come the potatoes and hump rib— grab hold!"

. 12 .

We were back on the river. Time began to move quickly now. The land sprawled and rolled into hills, that seemed to open to our advance, as if inviting us to enter.

We had paid the price and we made it, thanks mainly to the *voyageurs*, who had pulled and poled and rowed us up a river that defied us at every turn. At last we were free of the mosquitoes, ticks, and nettles that had tormented our flesh.

Along the Niobrara River the tangled cottonwoods thinned out, making the game visible and easy to shoot. Here I shot my first antelope, standing on a knoll while Potts lured the animal forward by waving a handkerchief tied to his gun barrel. I had heard that antelope were curious creatures and would even return to a place they had been frightened away from, if something aroused their curiosity. It was true.

The country kept changing, taking and giving by turn. It never stayed the same long enough for a man to become accustomed to it. We either had too much to eat or too little, and where there was meat, there were just as often hostile Indians. We had crept through Sioux country without incident, but the Creoles refused to work the towlines for fear of ambush, and the only men allowed off the boat were a handful of veterans who served as scouts. All of this slowed our progress, and the men were becoming edgy and short-tempered.

At last we reached the White River, and then, just above it, the Missouri Fur Company of Fort Recovery.

Once we crossed the Platte, the land was turned dry and flat, as if to defy our promised dream of mountains and meadows.

Major Henry, with his fowling piece, shot whatever birds he could—prairie hens, ducks, and occasionally a goose; and in the evenings Fink and Carpenter set out their lines, using bird gut for bait. Nearly every morning we had catfish to eat. But the few fish were not enough to go around, and there were days when there was no food at all to speak of.

In addition to the early deserters, we lost a handful of men at Fort Atkinson. At Fort Recovery we lost nine more. One of the men was Potts.

Potts didn't tell me himself; I got the news from Gardner. "What do you think of your friend deserting?" he said. I knew at once who he meant, but the shock was too much for me. I couldn't speak. I never had been sure if Potts was cut out to be a trapper, but I figured he'd find his way somehow or other once we reached the mountains.

I was half blaming myself when I went searching for him, hoping I could talk him into staying. "What will you do, Potts?" I asked when I had caught up with him. I could see he was upset, and I tried not to show my feelings so as not to upset him even more.

"I'm not rightly sure, Jim, but I won't starve to death, at least. Why don't you hang back, too? What're your prospects, anyhow?"

"No, Dan," I answered. "It's not for me to turn back. Not now. Not ever! There'll be tougher days than these, whether stayin' or leavin'. There's good diggin's ahead, and everyone knows it. Remember how we felt above the Platte, when we shot our first antelope and saw that herd of bufler from atop that hill—like a sea of rolling sagebrush—"

I talked on and on, but once a body like Potts gets an idea in his head, there ain't no way you can turn him around. Finally, there wasn't anything more to say. He had a notion to go to the mountains, but I had a dream, and that was the difference between us.

I walked Potts through the woods into a clearing where the only sound was a woodpecker drilling a hole into a dry tree stump. I helped him strap his pack while he looked off across the vast plain, through which he was headed—hoping for a better life, or at least an easier one than the life we had been sharing. Neither of us could say good-bye.

I stood motionless as he walked away and watched his figure grow smaller and smaller until it disappeared.

.13.

I'd never really known what a friend was before I had teamed up with Potts. Seems like I'd been alone all my life, and it looked like I was going to go on being alone.

As the days went by I found myself keeping my own company, while I concentrated my thoughts on getting up the river. I was feeling pretty low, but I was careful not to let it show. After all, we were a brigade, and a brigade can lose one or more of its members and still go on.

Several days out of Fort Recovery we came to Great Bend, a loop in the river that stretched forty miles long but only one mile across at its neck. In the time it would take for the keelboat to travel the loop, the land party was expected to shoot enough game to fill the empty stomachs of the crew.

The majority of the men had decided to hunt the shore along the neck, and so a handful of us, under Harris's orders, chose to work the riverbank, hoping to chase any game we couldn't shoot ourselves down to the men below us.

We hadn't worked the first mile of shoreline before we heard the crack of a rifle shot. We stood waiting for a second shot but none came.

"Let's see what that was," Harris ordered.

We found the men in a swale, crouched around an animal so large that from a distance I took it to be a grizzly.

"Good doin's," a voice at my side shouted. "It's bufler."

I had never seen a buffalo close-up before. I had always hoped that the first one I saw would be alive and positioned in the hind sights of my gun.

We formed a circle around the animal, which had already been planted down on its stomach, its four legs outspread. Gardner's knife flashed as he removed it from its sheath. He made a crosswise cut on the animal's neck and quickly separated the skin from the shoulder. The buffalo's head was facing me now, his beard trailing dust scraped from the ground. The eyes were still open, but the light had gone out of them. It was a noble head, large and black, with small, perfect horns and a broad, generous snout. After Gardner laid open the skin to the tail, he began peeling it down the sides.

"It ain't fat cow," Harris said at my side, "but it'll be good doin's for the likes of us. We'd best jerk some, I'm thinking."

"I'm making three cuttings," Gardner said. "One for keeping, one for eating now, and one for the Creoles. Who's for taking back the hindquarters?"

Harris stepped forward. "We'll need two men," he said, "to alternate and also to look out for game."

I stepped forward and took my place at his side.

"You and Bridger, then," Gardner said. As he spoke, he reached into the bloody cavity and pulled out the liver and gall bladder. Cutting the liver in two, he divided the larger half into three pieces. These he dipped in the gall bladder, and sticking one piece in his mouth, he tossed the other two pieces up—one to Harris, the other to me. "This'll hold you till you get back."

Harris greedily pushed his into his mouth, and I did the same. I had never eaten raw meat before. My mind recoiled at the same time that the muscles of my stomach reached out for the bounty.

There was more to this life than I knew or that ever got talked about. Though I didn't know what eating raw meat had to do with becoming a man, it had everything to do with being a mountaineer. That, and starving times, and all the rest. I hadn't come as far as I still had to go, that was certain.

.14.

From Great Bend we pushed on with renewed determination. There was a feeling now of hope. We knew there would be no more desertions, and we also knew that we needed all the men we had to reach our destination.

As if to test us one final time, the river showed still another side of itself, suddenly turning muscular and swift. The delta banks of mud had long ago given way to stony bluffs. Shoal followed rapid as the current grew fast and treacherous. We worked in shifts now, and for the first time some of us had to work the poles.

No one was exempt from duty. Those that didn't work the poles, or cordel, had to row.

One morning, as I was working at the sweeps, I suddenly noticed six Indians come riding toward us from behind a ridge. "Assiniboin," Talbot said at my side. "Friendlies."

Our men on horseback discharged their rifles in welcome salute. The Indians began shouting and waving their arms to demonstrate that they had come as friends. They rode up to our men and gesticulated and began talking in signs.

I continued to row, keeping my eyes on the water. Almost before I knew it, the channel changed course and began pulling our boat to the opposite shore. I noticed Major Henry out of the corner of my eye. He was standing atop the cargo box, eyeing the sail and looking anxiously up at the sky. His head suddenly jerked around. When I turned to follow his gaze, I saw what had caught his attention. Another party of Assiniboin was riding over a swale, straight toward our herd.

In an instant they completely surrounded our men and their fellow warriors. Our horses began whinnying, as a body of them broke loose from the herd, aroused by the Indians. They jostled each other as they fought to break loose.

All the men on the boat were standing now, helplessly watching. The Indians were riding between the band of frightened horses and the following guard. Suddenly the lead Indian raised his right arm and called out. All of the Indians instantly quirted their horses and waved their robes over their heads, making our loose horses stampede.

Our guard pulled up and tried to reload, but it was too late. By the time they raised their rifles to shoot, there was a cloud of dust between them and the Indians, who were now over the ridge and out of sight.

That night there was silence in our camp. We had traveled nearly two thousand miles in four and a half months. We had lost thirty-five horses and nearly as many men. And we had yet to reach the Yellowstone.

PART TWO

The Missouri Legion

1822–23

. 1 .

MAJOR HENRY CHOSE OUR SITE on a level strip of land a quarter of a mile above the confluence of the Missouri and Yellowstone rivers. It was late August when we disembarked and unloaded our cargo. The land was beginning to take on the burnished colors of autumn. The cottonwood groves were flecked in yellow, and the fallen leaves swirled in the gusts of cool wind that promised winter.

After we had arranged our supplies, Major Henry called us together, and drawing with a stick on the ground, he outlined the construction of our fort. It would consist of four small log huts connected by stockade walls.

We were divided into crews and assigned our jobs. We set to work at once. Harris and Gardner, with a small revolving crew, were to hunt and scout. Three groups were to fell the timber, snake the logs to the river, and frame the walls. I was put in charge of blacksmithing. I was to make hasps, hinges, handles, and nails, and also see that the saws and axes were kept sharpened.

The fort was completed by the middle of September. It was late in the afternoon of the final day of work that I walked off by myself to the confluence of the rivers. I sat on a rock, my back to the mountains that were too far away to see but that I knew loomed beyond the horizon. We hadn't made it to the Three Forks, but we had still come a piece. All we needed now was more horses and better weather. I lifted my eyes from the river and looked at Fort Henry. It wasn't nearly as noble a fort as the ones we had visited, but it was ours, built by our own hands and for our own purpose. It gave me a strong feeling of ownership and belonging.

Evening had come, and in the gathering stillness I listened to the river as it chirped and warbled—as if, like me, it had a life of its own and a destiny it was in touch with.

A white wolf appeared on a rise of land to my left, embraced by the vermilion glow of the setting sun. He raised his head in the direction of the river and howled mournfully. He stood as if frozen, his head upturned, his tail curled down between his legs. It seemed to me he was calling, not to the river but to me, the intruder.

That evening the trapping crews were arranged, and the following morning we fanned out in parties of two or more to work all of the streams. Twelve men elected to go off to the Musselshell Basin two hundred miles distant. Included in this brigade were Fink, Carpenter, and Talbot. Fink had decided he would stay and trap. His career as a boatman had apparently come to an end. The *voyageurs* had already returned with the keelboat to St. Louis.

I was picked to go with Johnson Gardner. All parties were to trap within the vicinity of the fort, meeting at intervals to report progress and count noses.

"We don't expect to encounter Blackfeet this time of year," Major Henry said as the men readied their rigging. "But this is their territory, and you never know when you're apt to come upon a roving band. We haven't seen any signs, and my guess is they've gone north to hunt buffalo."

We were issued ball and powder, a horn containing musk or castor of beaver, and six traps each, with a trap sack to carry them in.

"So you'll be floating your stick with mine," Gardner said as we walked off together. We crossed the icy river and wound our way through the timber. Gardner led our horse, which was loaded down with our traps and the equipment we'd need for making camp.

"You'd better hope those moccasins that squaw sold you back at Fort Atkinson were made from the skin of last winter's lodge," Gardner said as we threaded our way through a cottonwood grove.

I didn't know what he meant, but before I could ask, he continued.

"You'll know if they start pinching," he said, the corners of his mouth turning up in a grin.

"Oh," I said, suddenly catching on, "they need to be smoked to keep them from shrinking."

Gardner snorted his approval. "We're a bragging lot," he said after a long silence, "given to tall tales and swagger. And why not! We've earned it. Most go under, that's the truth. But it's worth it if you're cut out for this life.

"If'n you want to keep your scalp, you'll learn, fast and certain, 'cause one mistake may be too many. I'm not goin' to brag on you this trip. I'm goin' to do you like I was done by. If you learn, and if you're lucky, you'll make the grade. You look to have the makings, and I'm going to show you all I can.

"Don't forget anything I tell you, 'cause I may not say it twice. A trapper can learn a lot by watching bufler or elk graze—or even by the behavior of little critters. You can read things in their movements, same as a stick or branch floating down a stream may be a sign of beaver or Injuns, or maybe somethin' else.

"There's grizzly and pois'n snakes and Blackfeet. . . ." His voice trailed off as he studied the land at the farthest end of the meadow we had entered. "There—over there," he said, pointing. "Trapping's a trade like any other, but it's tougher than any other trade and more rewarding—'cause we're free! We're cussed but we're free!"

58

We were halfway across the meadow. The land opened in all directions from where we stood. The sky was the biggest I had ever seen, and the flowing, marshy grass, that blew in waves, silver and golden-green, was like a sea without a shore, except for the sky that seemed to hold the land in place.

A circling eagle swooped down to have a better look at us and then flew off, growing smaller and smaller until he was a distant, colorless point in the blue sky.

"Best time to trap's just before sundown, working hard to full dark. Six traps takes up a piece, but you have to get 'em all in no matter how."

Water the color of glass came into sight. A beaver lodge appeared in a stream that had been dammed to make a pond.

"A beaver can't see moving water without wanting to put a stop to it," Gardner said, smiling. "They have their ways." I could see he was fond of the creatures. They were all the excuse he had—or needed—to be able to live the life of a mountain man. It was a good enough reason to be fond of them.

"Know why we trap in the fall?" Gardner asked. We were within one hundred yards of the lodge now. "We'll trap that pond last, it's still early." He turned as he spoke, and we began walking downriver.

"Pelts are prime in autumn," I said, answering his question.

"Prime plews in spring," he said. "That's not the

reason. They wander off to the fields in summer, to forage like rabbits—carefree as you like. Squaw beaver expecting families stay put, but not the rest. They'll all be returning about now to get ready for the long winter."

We worked our way downstream, leaving the meadow and plunging into a cottonwood thicket that gave way to a field of buffalo grass. We could follow the curve of the stream by the trees growing along the bank.

At the edge of the wood we jumped three deer that quietly disappeared over a swale, their white tails like flags waving good-bye.

"Bufler be coming down soon," Gardner said, "but no shooting this trip, not till we're sure the territory's free of Injuns. There'll be signs if'n there are any. Best be careful."

We crept toward the setting sun, a slight breeze in our faces. Entering the stream, we stood for a moment in respect for the quiet we had disturbed. Our movement sent ripples across the water toward the opposite bank.

"Where we gonna put these traps?" Gardner asked.

"Slide bottoms, or along the drag paths," I said, my eye following the route the beaver had taken in making their lodge.

Gardner switched the plug in his mouth before spitting. "We make 'em come to medicine," he said, cocking his head in my direction. "I'll show you."

He had already set his trap as we worked our way back to the shore. Now he placed his trap in shallow water, driving a stick through the ring and into the streambed. Pulling the stopper of his horn with his teeth, he dipped a stripped branch into the medicine. The musky smell rose to my nostrils, making me recoil.

"Once you get used to it, you'll wonder why the townsfolk shy away when they greet you. Till you remember," he added, smiling.

He planted his stick in the bank, just above the trap. Then he moved the float attached to the stick by a chain as far out into the stream as it would go.

"We catch 'em with their own scent," he said, pointing to the dipped stick on the bank. "Their musk is the stuff they mark their territories with. One of 'em's sure to swim out here to check on the smell, and this trap'll catch his back paw, just slick. You place the stick high if'n you want to catch his hind foot, and low if'n you want to catch the forefoot."

I wanted to know what would happen once the beaver caught his leg. "He'll dive for the bottom when he's caught," Gardner explained. "Water's too deep here for him to get back up. With the trap and stake holding him down, he'll drown."

"You need a good set to the stick, then."

"That's it!"

As we backed away he threw sprays of water on the bank to cover our scent and his footprints.

We set our sixth trap below the meadow we had crossed earlier in the day. The eagle that had returned to watch was still barely visible, silhouetted on a bluff above the silky meadow.

.2.

We made cold camp that night and set out early the following morning to check our traps. My buckskin trousers and moccasins still felt a little damp, but my moccasins hadn't shrunk. I looked down at them, wondering about the tepee they had come from.

"Best to get moving," Johnson said, interrupting my thoughts. "Fire won't warm us like traveling will."

Gardner undid the *par flèche* with which we had hobbled our horse the night before. He rubbed her lowered head and spoke into her ear. She snorted, blowing twin plumes of smoke into the air. A shaft of sunlight blazed through the surrounding stand of trees where we had made our camp, lighting the drops of dew that dripped from the leaves and clung to the knobs of branches.

It took less time to collect our traps than it had to set them. We caught five beaver in all, but one of them, having cut the float, dived to the middle of the dam before drowning.

Gardner had to dive for beaver and trap. When he surfaced, he said, simply, "Wood too green." He stepped ashore, his buckskins dripping water.

"That's fifty-pound beaver, sure," I said. "Didn't know they came that large."

"I've seen 'em even bigger." Gardner was holding the beaver by the tail. "If'n they're this big, they'll pull the stake loose on you more'n half the time."

There were beaver in all the other traps but one, where we found a hind foot that a beaver had chewed off to get himself free. Gardner cursed under his breath but didn't make any excuses. I wanted to ask what had gone wrong, but when he didn't volunteer to tell me, I figured it was something that couldn't be easily explained. It was something I would have to learn on my own.

After releasing the severed foot of the beaver he let it fall to the ground before kicking it aside, as if he were annoyed with something—the beaver, himself, I couldn't tell. A man could lose his stomach for this business, I thought, if this kind of thing happened too often.

We picked a safe spot for camp, where we would have a good lookout, although by now we were pretty sure there weren't any Indians in the area.

After we'd cut some fine shavings, making a loose

mound, Gardner took his flint and steel from his bullet pouch, along with some punk that I had seen him scoop out of a dead tree. He struck fire into the punk and placed it in a nest that he had bunched into shape from a handful of dead grass. In an instant it blazed, and adding dry wood to our shavings, we soon had a good fire, over which we began cooking our coffee.

As soon as the coals were hot, Gardner cut off one of the beaver tails and threw it into the fire. "Good doin's," he said. "Just peel and eat. This child knows he's in the mountains when he eats his first beaver tail of the season."

And good doin's it was. I was trying to think of something to compare it to. "Fine as hump rib," I said at last.

"Some says better," Gardner answered. "I'll say this much, lots eats bufler, only the trappers eat beaver tail."

We threw in another tail. This one I skinned myself.

"You've gotta put something inside that six feet of yours," Johnson said, as I dished him some of the tail.

"Tell me more about beaver," I said.

"They've got smarts, certain," Gardner began, leaning back comfortably against a tree. "Once they're up to trap, pick up and move on, is what I says. If'n you're a stubborn cuss, you'll fight 'em, placing your traps in drag paths like you said, but your beaver'll spring them with a stick. Next you wanta put the traps bottom upwards, or conceal 'em in mud. But nothing works. I know! I've tried! If'n they're up to trap, then this coon's not up to beaver.

"Now, there's hard doin's and easy doin's. Ever heard tell of bachelors? What the French call *les parrasseux*. They don't go in for families, dams, or lodges. No, siree! They burrow themselves a tunnel. Sometimes there be several in one 'abode,' which makes for good pickin's, 'cause bachelors are the easiest beaver to trap."

"They must be something like us," I said.

That one got Gardner good. He slapped his knee and let out a bellow. Slapping his knee caused his beaver tail to fly back into the fire. "If'n that don't beat all!" he exclaimed. "You're the first to say it, I've heard. No families, no lodges, and no pond life to speak of. Hi-ya!"

"Don't take much to catch us, neither."

Gardner stabbed his meat back out of the fire. "You've got young grit and a meat bag full of good wit," he said. "You're ready to start trappin' alone— maybe tonight. But first I'll have to larn you to stretch and cure skins."

. 3 .

We'd been out trapping about a month when we were called back to the fort by the sounding of the swivel.

Gardner and I stood and watched as the puff of smoke rose and dissolved in the cold blue sky. "That'll be Ashley," Gardner observed.

"Could just be announcing their arrival," I said. "Not necessarily calling us in."

"I aim to know the news," Gardner answered. "Besides which, they may be fixin' to haul our cache down to St. Louis."

"Won't they wait till the season's over?"

" 'Bout over now. Those gumbos aren't going to hang around for the Injuns to show up. Anyways, let's pack our pelts and head in. This beaver's half froze for a drink. Whataya figure the day is?"

"About the middle of October."

"Season's used up, then, just about."

It was midday when we reached the fort, the day's skins still wet and needing curing. Our horse, that we had named Red, whinnied and shook her head when the fort came into sight.

"Misses her stallion," Johnson said. "Can't wait to see the herd. Not so different from us, I'm thinking."

Gardner's first guess was right. Ashley's keelboat had arrived. What we hadn't known was that Ashley's other party had arrived two weeks earlier, on mounts purchased from the Rees. His party consisted of some of the veterans we had read about in Franklin, including a man named Jedediah Smith. The keelboat consisted mostly of raw recruits, greenhorns like myself, but it also contained a very big surprise—Dan Potts!

Potts was sitting in front of the stockade, looking out over the river, dreamily pulling on his pipe, when we pulled in. I didn't recognize him until he sprang to his feet and shouted my name. "Hey-ya, Bridger, you old coon!"

I was too stunned to speak. I just stood there, gawking at him. And then we both ran forward and threw our arms around each other. "I didn't know if you'd gone under," I said, catching my breath, "or found your way back to St. Louis—or what."

Potts just looked me up and down and then shook his head to indicate that he'd been through a trial or two.

We walked through the gates of the fort, our arms around each other's shoulders. "I signed back on with Ashley at Fort Atkinson," Potts began. "I was half dead when I got there, I don't mind telling you. Starved crossing the prairie. I was all alone. Lost my possibles, then some Injuns took me in—"

"Slow down."

"It ain't worth dwellin' on, anyways," Potts said. "I'm here, ain't I? And tickled to be alive. This is the rarest country a body ever put eyes to. We've seen herds of bufler from the boat like nothing I ever dreamed of. This is new land, Jim, brand-new land, I tell ya. Not spoilt, like the States is a'ready. I'll never go back to the settlements, now I've seen this."

I nodded my head in agreement. He was sure a sight for sore eyes. I was staring at his hair for some reason, that he had braided into a single tail that fell down his back. Mine had grown, too, but I preferred to let it hang loose over my shoulders. It made me realize how long it had been since we'd seen each other.

"I'd like to get back someday to see my sister," I said, "to make sure she's all right. And I aim to send her money soon as I can. Otherwise, I'm bound for the mountains, I am."

"Let's have a drink," Potts said. "You must be powerful dry."

"I'm half froze for a shot of Monongohela," I said.

"Jim Bridger, you have the right good manners of a fur-trappin' man!" Potts said, and gave out a holler. I followed with a hoot of my own as we headed for the company store.

Old Potts was sure a sight for sore eyes. He sure was.

.4.

On the morning of our second day back in camp, General Ashley and Major Henry began interviewing the men. In addition to assignments, there was the new supply of goods to be distributed.

A small party had already gone up the Yellowstone to make some meat for the fort and to trap whatever beaver they could. The party included Jedediah Smith, the bible-toter that Potts had been keen to tell me about. "He's young like you, Jim. You'll get on slick, I'll lay," Potts had said.

Ashley and Henry wanted twenty-one more men to bolster the Musselshell Brigade. The leader would be a veteran by the name of Captain Weber. Potts had pointed him out to me. He was powerfully built and tall, with an erect carriage. I liked the look of him.

In addition to those two parties, there was going to be a Missouri contingent that Major Henry would see as far as the Milk River.

We all understood the nature and the urgency of these maneuvers. Between the loss of the keelboat *Enterprize* and the arrival of Ashley's crew on horseback, a detachment of forty-three men of the Missouri Fur Company had arrived at the fort. They were led by Jones and Immell, Joshua Pilcher's lieutenants. They were on their way up the Yellowstone to winter at the Big Horn. We treated them with hospitality, just as we had been treated at all the forts we had stopped at, even though they were our competitors and were working the same region we planned to work come spring.

Both of our companies wanted to get near the Three Forks as soon as possible. I was hoping to go with either of the parties; it didn't matter which. I wanted to get to the mountains, and if that meant fighting Indians, I was ready.

Once again I was standing before General Ashley. We smiled at each other in recognition. I didn't feel as nervous as I had the last time we spoke. I'd come a piece, and I felt I could do the work of any man, if given half a chance.

"You don't look as lean and green as you did in the spring, Bridger," General Ashley said. "A season on the Missouri can do wonders for a man—one way or another." He glanced around the room, but when he didn't see what he was hunting for, he turned back to me. I couldn't be sure, but I had a notion he was thinking of Potts, not to mention all the deserters who never came back.

"I hear you've taken to trapping beaver like a duck to new water. Old Gardner says you held your own with him, beaver for beaver. As soon as we build that pirogue and the first hunters get back, I'm taking our packs back to St. Louis. You've made yourself some money. Maybe you'd like to come back with me and spend it."

"No, sir!" I blurted out.

General Ashley smiled. "That's a right smart flintlock you got there. Hawken, same as mine. You'll be putting it to good use making meat for camp this winter. That's all to the good, Jim, but there's something else I'll be needing you for as well."

I lowered my gun, the bull banging noisily on the floor. I was hoping the general hadn't noticed my disappointment.

"You're a blacksmith," he went on, "and your skills are needed. I brought a real forge with me, along with the tools you'll need and enough iron. We'll be needing lots of things. In particular, traps. We left St. Louis before I could purchase any. The manufacturers aren't able to keep up with the demand. The ones we have now will have to go out with Captain Weber and Major Henry. The traps you make we'll use in the spring. Can you do it?"

"Yes, sir," I said. "Whatever is needed, I'll do it, best I can."

"There'll be some veterans staying behind, for you to learn from. I haven't forgotten what you told me when you signed on back in St. Louis. You want to work and you want to learn. Is that right?"

"That's right, sir. How about Potts, sir? Will he be staying or leaving?"

"He'll be with Major Henry's bunch. You'll see them on the Musselshell come spring."

Once I got used to the idea, it felt good to be among the men that remained to mind the fort. I had work to keep me occupied day after day, whereas the hunting parties were often confined to the fort with nothing to do, once the winter snows set in. Fortunately, an occasional stray buffalo would find our fort and use our walls for a wind break, providing us with fresh meat through the hardest months.

All in all it proved to be a good winter. But I sure never thought I'd travel two thousand miles and still not be in the mountains, or that I would give up the trade I had learned in the States only to have it thrust upon me out here. Life never seemed to turn out the way you expected. There was a lesson in that, I was sure, but it wasn't an easy lesson to learn.

By the end of March the ice began to break on the river. The Missouri went over its banks, and the Yellowstone backed up water; while endless hunks of ice, some carrying rabbits, wildcats, and other frightened creatures, went skimming downriver past our stockade.

The fort began to fill with men now. Potts was among the first group to arrive, having been severely wounded in both knees by an accidental discharge of a rifle while they were trapping the Judith River. He had arrived while I was out on a scouting expedition on the Missouri River led by Major Henry. Before we reached our destination, we had been repulsed by a band of Blackfoot Indians who had killed four of our men.

Poor Potts. He sure had a talent for trouble. I had hoped all along that he could have stayed the winter in the fort—not only because he was good company,

but because I figured he'd get seasoned by talking to
the veterans, going out on short hunts, and so on—
and then, too, he might have worked along with me
in the forge, though he didn't seem to have much of a
hankering for blacksmithing. Well, a body had to
work and learn—and you had to know what you were
aiming for; otherwise, you were like a straw in the
wind, and every time the weather changed, your life
would just up and change with it.

Potts was awaiting my arrival once again. I found
him in the blacksmith shop examining my work.
He looked up to see me standing in the doorway.
"Jedediah brought me back to the fort in your canoe,"
Potts said. "He also whittled this cane for me." I
could tell he was feeling funny about the way he
looked.

"Bad luck seems to trail you like a hound," I said.
"When will you be able to throw that stick away?"

"Soon! Real soon! I'll have a limp, though. Didn't
mend straight, but it'll be all right. I'll get on."

"Hope you're not planning to go back to St. Louis
in the fall."

"I'm sticking it out this time, Jim. Don't have nothing to go back for anymore, just like you."

"We're paddling the same canoe," I said. I walked
up to Potts and slapped him on the back. "You're a
sight for sore eyes, partner."

"And you likewise."

We walked together out of the blacksmith shop and into the compound. Potts took out his pipe. He placed his full weight on his cane while he reached his pipe inside his tobacco pouch. "You notice any faces missing?" he asked, packing tobacco into the bowl with his thumb.

I looked around the compound and then back at Potts.

"Carpenter and Fink fell out on the Musselshell over some squaw. Must've been some crib girl back in the settlements, 'cause we didn't see any women-folk—white or Injun—all the time we was there.

"Anyhow, they patched it up, I heard, before they came back. I was hobbling pretty bad then, but news of one of their famous shootin' matches reached my ears in time, and I got out to the yard just as the copper was skyed.

"Mike won the toss." Potts paused and placed his pipe in his mouth before hobbling over to a bench and sitting down. I joined him and waited for the rest of the story.

"Apparently they had just had another quarrel over the squaw, and Fink decided after they patched it up that they would shoot the cups just to show there wasn't bad blood between them.

"We learned later that Carpenter whispered to Talbot after the toss that Mike intended to kill him. He bequeathed his rifle and pistol to Talbot before marching off with his cup.

"He didn't look to me like a man about to lose his life, I'll tell you that. He stood tall, with no change in his expression that I could see.

"Well, Mike leveled his rifle and drew a bead. Then he pulled his iron down and says to Carpenter, right smart—a smile on his lips—'Hold your noodle steady, Carpenter, and don't spill the whiskey, as I shall want some presently.' Then again he raised his iron, and this time he shot, almost without aiming, it seemed. Carpenter didn't make a sound. He just fell forward on his face. Fink had shot him in the forehead, right between the eyes. The back of his head was missing.

"Just as casual as can be," Potts continued, "Mike set the breech of his gun on the ground and, putting his mouth to the muzzle, blew the smoke out of the barrel. Finally he said, 'Carpenter, you have spilled the whiskey.'

"'You killed him intentional,' Talbot roared at Fink.

"'It's all a mistake,' Fink answered, 'for I took as fine a bead on the black spot on the cup as I ever took on a squirrel's eye. How did it happen?'

"Then he commenced to curse his rifle, the bullets, and finally himself."

"That can't be the end of it," I said.

"No, that wasn't the finish of it, not by a long chalk. A couple weeks later Fink, in a fit of drunken boasting, claimed he killed Carpenter on purpose and was glad of it. The words were hardly out of his mouth when Talbot whipped out the pistol Carpenter had bequeathed him and shot Fink in the heart. Fink fell forward, same as Carpenter had done. He was dead when he hit the ground."

"I wonder what's for Talbot?"

"Don't know," Potts said. "Help me up, Jim, my knees are cramping something awful."

.5.

We were ready to leave Fort Henry to make our assault on the mountains and to begin our life of trapping. I couldn't help but feel that that winter had been a hard but necessary preparation for the spring.

"You're a *hivernan* now," Gardner said to me one day. "You've wintered, and that means you've been accepted by the land and the trade."

All I could answer in reply was that I felt different. I guess I felt that I had earned my spurs.

Major Henry called a meeting one evening after mess, and I was invited. Except for me it seemed to be a pretty select crowd. The meeting began with the topic that was on everyone's mind. "We all know we're in need of horses. Our aim is to trap the Three Forks come fall the latest. We're going to miss the spring season, we know that already." Major Henry paused and looked around the room.

Harris was the first to speak. "We won't get far up the Big Horn, the Tongue, or even the Powder River without pack animals."

"Are you assuming we can't make Three Forks this year?" Major Henry asked. The room became silent as everyone turned their attention toward Harris.

"No, I'm just saying we'll need more horses than we've got even to get partway there."

"Even if we're not equipped, we can leastways get out of Blackfoot country," Gardner said. "Isn't that the important thing?"

"The Crows'll be friendly," Captain Weber put in. "We can count on a change of luck if we get that far."

"It's too risky," Major Henry said, "and we've got too much at stake. I need a courier to get a message to General Ashley. It seems to me the general is our only hope for horses."

Jedediah was the first to volunteer. "I'll go," he said simply. "I know the country and I can make good time."

"It'll take two," Major Henry said. "You don't want to go out in this country alone. Not if you can help it."

I was ready to go, but for some reason I was afraid to speak up. Major Henry glanced around the room. His gaze rested on me for a split second, and I knew he had read the willing expression on my face. "I'll need a veteran," he said. Turning, he let his attention rest on Gardner. "How about it, Johnson, you know the country and the situation as well as anyone here." Gardner slowly nodded his head, while Major Henry continued. "Tell the general a good horse in the Rockies will cost us upwards of a hundred and fifty dollars. That's twice what the same horse would cost in St. Louis.

"It would be good if we could trade with the Crows," he continued, looking at Weber, "but they'd rather buy horses than sell them. Our only hope is the Rees."

Turning back to Gardner and Smith, he said, "You should be able to contact Ashley before he reaches the Arikara Villages."

"You're assuming the Rees are going to be friendly," Gardner said.

"I'm not assuming, I'm hoping."

"You never know from day to day with the Rees," Weber said.

Major Henry looked at Weber and then back to Gardner and Smith. "Tell the general that if we decide to try for the Three Forks again, we'll need to follow the Yellowstone, not the Missouri, and that means crossing the mountains. Forty horses won't be too many."

That was where the meeting ended. It was decided

Smith and Gardner would leave in two days. I was disappointed by the delay. But at the same time I was grateful. In the condition Potts was in, he'd never get to the mountains, especially if we were short of mounts. It now looked like we'd be able to borrow the time he would need.

.6.

Jedediah had returned—on foot. General Ashley had been routed by the Rees. After trading for horses they had been decoyed onto the sandbar directly below the lower village. The Indians had killed fifteen men and wounded nine more. Jedediah narrowly escaped with his life. Gardner was among the wounded.

Major Henry went into action at once. Our forty-man company was divided in two. Half would remain with Captain Weber to protect the fort, while the rest of us would join General Ashley. "This trapping life is sure full of surprises," I said to Potts while putting my rigging together. "I guess you'll have to hold down the fort till we get back."

"Do you wish sometimes you were back in St. Louis, knowing what you'd be doing from day to day? Everything nice and safe."

"And nothing ever new. No thanks."

We were both smiling. Despite the danger and uncertainty, we didn't have any doubts or regrets.

"We're a team," I said. "All of us! That's what this life does for a man. You're alone and free—the way you could never be in the States—and yet you are a part of something bigger, something you don't even understand.

"I wish you were coming, Potts. It's going to be a show."

"You teach them Rees a lesson. I sure wish I could be at your side for this one."

"There'll be plenty more," I answered. "Just wait'll we return and get ourselves to the mountains."

We joined General Ashley at the mouth of the Cheyenne River, where he waited with the men, keelboats, and goods that had been salvaged from the attack. Forty-three men had deserted him, but when Colonel Leavenworth of Fort Atkinson got word of the problem, he took command on his own authority, since it would take too long to receive official orders. He mustered six companies of the Sixth Infantry, totaling two hundred and thirty officers and men, and made ready to march on the enemy.

The Missouri Fur Company was also prepared. They contributed between forty and fifty men, and two keelboats, which brought the number of keelboats to five.

Now, for the first time, we learned that the same Blackfoot war party that had killed four of our men on the upper Missouri had also wiped out seven men of the Missouri Fur Company. They had also lost an entire season's work in furs.

Bolstered by Colonel Leavenworth's confidence, and Ashley and Pilcher's resolve, twenty of our deserters rejoined the company, which now numbered eighty strong. In addition, hundreds of Sioux warriors were recruited, all of them eager to deal a death blow to their long-standing enemies, the Arikaras.

By the end of June we had begun our charge up the Missouri River, as strange a mixture of men as one could imagine: fur trappers, Indians, soldiers, and officers, marching on land and being carried over water in five keelboats armed with two six-pounders and a five-and-a-half-inch howitzer.

Jedediah Smith was named captain of our company, which included several men that I would come to know better as time went on: Thomas Fitzpatrick, Jim Clyman, Bill Sublette, and Thomas Eddie.

We were six weeks on the river before we reached a strategic point below the Arikara Villages.

At last we were ready to go into battle. I felt nervous for the first time when ammunition was distributed and our arms were checked. The Sioux warriors were given strips of white muslin to wrap around their heads so they could be distinguished from the Rees.

A small band of warriors was sent ahead of the troops to engage the Rees on their own territory. The strategy was simple, and it worked. When the Rees saw the Sioux approaching, they left their villages and met them on the battlefield, thus exposing themselves to the advancing army.

A company of riflemen followed the warriors, while our two companies trailed behind. Four companies of infantry followed us, with the remaining Sioux in the rear and on the flanks.

Several minutes passed without a sound. Then we heard the war cries of Indians, followed by clouds of ascending dust that told us the battle had begun.

Because the Sioux had galloped ahead of us on their mounts, it was an hour before we entered the plain where the fighting was taking place. "It looks more like a swarm of bees than a battlefield of men," a voice in front of me said. It belonged to Jim Clyman, one of the lucky survivors of the Arikara battle. The Indians on the flats were running and riding and hurling themselves upon one another, all the while yelling their war cries.

Leavenworth quickly maneuvered his troops into position, placing us and the other riflemen on the flanks with the infantry in the middle. But with Indians scattered and intermixed across the wide sweep of land before us, it was impossible for us to fire, as we would be certain to kill as many Sioux as Rees.

As we approached, the Arikaras began retreating to their villages. We kept moving forward until we were within gun range, where we halted and looked around, uncertain of what to do next.

"We've treed the coon," Fitzpatrick called out to Jedediah, who was now Captain Smith.

"It may not be as easy to shoot him out of the branches," Jedediah replied, "as it was to get him up the trunk."

. 7 .

There were dead Indians lying along the plain. Among the bodies, I made out muslin headbands belonging to the two Sioux warriors who had been killed. There must have been ten to fifteen fallen Rees, some of them still alive. As the wounded Sioux were being removed from the field, other warriors were cutting up the dead bodies of the Rees. I had to struggle not to turn away. They were attaching cords to dismembered arms, legs, hands, and feet and dragging them along the ground. This was their triumph. They were rejoicing in their victory.

"C'mon," Jedediah said, grabbing my arm.

"It's hideous," I said.

"Let's go, then. You don't have to watch."

Jedediah turned and walked away, following the rest of the men who were leaving the field. Out of the corner of my eye I noticed an old Sioux chief walking with a squaw toward the fallen body of one of the Rees. When they reached the body, the chief handed the squaw a club, with which she began pummeling the body of the dead brave, while the chief taunted the Rees for their cowardice in having fled the field of battle.

I had seen enough, but as I turned to walk away I saw an old Sioux coming forward on his hands and knees toward the body of a dead Ree. He was wrapped in the skin of a grizzly bear, his head inside its head, the grizzly's teeth crowning his forehead. He had a rattle in his left hand, and he was naked to his breechcloth. His body was painted differently from the other warriors. As he drew close to the Ree he began snorting and then mimicked a bear by snarling and contorting his face, while with his teeth he tore the flesh from the breast of the dead body.

The other Sioux were averting their eyes and begged those of us who were looking on to turn away so as not to disturb the power of the grizzly-bear medicine.

I left the scene and began walking toward the river. Day was ending at last. A party of men had formed on the beach, out of gun range of the lower town, resting and waiting for rations, although we had run out of food two days before. Perhaps someone would shoot a deer or antelope, or even a turkey—if they hadn't been scattered to the winds by the howling and fighting and "medicine acts." I sat down against a log and looked out at the river.

I must have dozed off. When I awoke, it was dark. A campfire had been lit, the hot coals reflected in the faces of the men around me. I realized that I had had a nightmare. I was remembering images of torn flesh and contorted, agonized bodies, with mouth after mouth forming in frozen circles of sound, from which screams and wailing and sobs issued, finally ending in a solitary wail.

Then I heard the firing of guns and yelling, and I knew for certain that I was awake. A hand reached toward me from the fire and handed me a piece of meat, but when I raised it to my mouth, the smell that rose to my nostrils was the stench of dead bodies.

The human wailing, that was slowly subsiding, was being taken up by the howling of dogs and braying of horses and mules. The last sound I remember before falling asleep again was the hooting of an owl.

.8.

The next day was spent in pounding the villages with artillery. The first explosion from the six-pounder killed their chief, Grey Eyes. The Sioux warriors stormed off almost at once, disgusted with the white man's way of fighting. They told Pilcher, "The white chief is an old woman. He makes his war in the air. We are warriors, we fight on the ground, with our weapons in our hands, and when we count coup, it is with our enemy, that we have engaged hand to hand. A warrior captures horses and kills the enemy, he does not destroy tepees and lodges and hide from the enemy."

The soldiers wanted to attack, but Colonel Leavenworth wouldn't move without Sioux support. He wanted to negotiate, but that only infuriated his men. Captain Riley raged. "We've been at garrison at Council Bluffs for ten years, eating nothing but pumpkins, and now when there is a small chance for promotion, it is denied us."

Suddenly it occurred to me that *everyone* was crazy. Pilcher wanted to teach the Rees a lesson. As far as he was concerned, a negotiated peace was a cowardly form of defeat. But how could there be victory in war, or peace in killing? Had everyone gone mad?

That night it was quiet on the beach. There was a feeling that passed among us that the Rees had fled, leaving us alone with the buried dead, the empty villages, and our own cause, that had no purpose now, if in fact it ever had had one. It was a feeling of defeat I felt, and I seemed to be sharing it in some form or other with the others. We waited for morning to break. I kept to myself. I had no wish to speak to anyone.

The colonel, after taking his breakfast, could think of nothing better to do than wander through the abandoned villages, to see what damage he had inflicted with his cannonballs. Only one Indian remained behind, Chief Grey Eyes' aged mother, who was left in the company of forty dogs and a lone rooster. The army gave her water and rations and left her in possession of the towns. The colonel, with his men, returned to the beach and set off downriver toward Fort Atkinson.

Their boats had hardly turned the first bend in the river when a few men from the Missouri Fur Company slipped back into the villages and set them aflame.

I crossed the river, alone, and climbed atop a rock ledge from where I had a commanding view of the river and the plain. The smoke was beginning to billow from the villages. There was no visible fire, except for occasional flashes of flame that were soon swallowed by the smoldering smoke.

I sat down on the rocks and watched the keelboat turn a final bend and disappear. I stood up and looked at the smoking villages. I would not quit and go back to the States, as most of the men had decided to do. I was going to achieve my dream. This land belonged to the man who loved it—no less the white man than the Indian.

PART THREE

Blanket Chief

1823–24

.1.

POTTS HAD THROWN AWAY his cane. He wasn't going to be a cripple, after all. As he moved forward to greet me and the rest of our returning party, I noticed only the faintest hint of a drag in his left leg, caused by a hitch in the knee.

"You look like the bona fide article," I said to Potts, after we had embraced. He had grown a full beard, and there was an eagle feather stuck in his cap that was made of fur and leather flap.

"I wasn't worried about whether I'd see you again," Potts said, and laughed. "Not after news reached us of your comic-opera affair with the Rees. Saved your hair at the expense of your pride, looks like."

"How's it been here?" I asked, changing the subject.

"We've lost twenty some horses, but we can't lay the blame on you—excepting that we didn't have enough men to guard our mounts. It's those durn Blackfeet."

"So we've lost at both ends."

"Maybe so," Potts answered, pulling at his sandy beard. "You had a long trek from the looks of it. Just enough horses for packing. Feet must be sore, I'll lay. Good thing I traded for some moccasins while you were gone. I've got a pair that'll fit you in my fixin's."

"How would you like to walk down to where the rivers join up?" I asked. "There's a good stone to sit on there, and a view of the country. These bones need some quiet for a spell."

"Let me fetch my iron," Potts said. "You go on."

I had reached the rock ahead of Potts and moved over to make room for him when he walked up. "This is a mighty fine situation," I said. "First time I sat here, a white wolf came up that bluff and howled at me real powerful."

"Telling you to go home, I reckon. Lots have, that we came up with. Someone said another band of men are heading west. Must be Jed Smith's with that party."

"Leading it, I would say. Sixteen in number, if I'm not mistaken. Tom Fitzpatrick, Bill Sublette, Jim Clyman, Thomas Eddie. Some real mountaineers in the making. They were waiting for horses when we left Fort Kiowa."

"What made you drop down there?"

"That's where Ashley stored his provisions. The great battle left us embarrassed and disgusted—and hungry. About the only thing we managed to do was chase the game away from the river."

"You came back with only eleven men. How about the others?"

"A few were killed; the others went back to St. Louis with Ashley. Those men with Smith, they're talking about becoming free trappers. Sell to whomever they like. If no one's gonna protect the territory, then they're not gonna be beholdin'—"

"I ain't ready to float my stick alone—"

"We don't have to—yet! But I'm thinking, a white man can't keep his hair long in these diggin's less'n he's able to take care of himself. First of all, we have to know everything concerning Injun ways. The real mountaineers—they're more Injun than white—but the red man's their sworn enemy. The way I look at it, there's room for everyone."

"Looks like you've been doing a lot of thinking," Potts said, reaching inside his buckskin jacket. "Here, try these moccasins on. The ones on your feet look about finished."

"We'll need to go trapping now," I said as I ran my hand over the beads. "We're gonna need something to trade with this winter."

"Autumn comes early to these diggin's," Potts said in response. "It's time to move on, I reckon."

"I'm thanking you for the moccasins, Dan."

.2.

Potts and I were floating our sticks together again, this time under Captain Weber, with whom we were selected to travel, along with a handful of others, up the Powder River. Major Henry's party, which consisted of more than half the remaining men, was to travel up the Yellowstone to the Big Horn River. Our two parties planned to meet up with the Smith brigade somewhere in Crow country, where we would set up winter quarters. We were all that remained of the Ashley–Henry Company, and now at last we were going to the mountains. Each man had his own mount, and two packhorses as well. We started out at mid-morning on a clear, windless day.

"It sure is different traveling by horse," I said to Potts. "Makes a man feel equipped somehow."

Potts and I were riding side by side over a hogback ridge, our eye on the line of timber that stood between us and the river.

"Only two other ways to travel," Potts answered, "boat and on your own hoof. But all ways take their own learning. You take your Injun, he can do all three about equal."

"I guess it will be Gardner and Harris traveling ahead, making meat for the rest of the party."

"I reckon. They're the best qualified, being they know the country."

"I'd like to have a chance sometime."

"It won't be a day or two before we'll all be trapping," Potts said.

It was sundown before we caught up with the hunters. Gardner and Harris were busy cutting up an elk they had shot. "Where'd you down it?" Captain Weber asked when we reached them.

"Dry-wash hollow east of here," Gardner said. "You hear the shooting?"

Captain Weber shook his head. "Soon as you're done, we'll move ahead and make camp." We rode till we were in sight of the river, with Captain Weber in advance selecting a site for our camp.

Gardner pulled up at my side as our mounts came to a halt. "You watch how it's done," he said, looking at me and Potts. "It's different making camp with horses, especially in hostile country—and Captain Weber won't be fooling, he's got a military mind, you'll see. Just watch."

We dismounted and removed our packs and saddles at once, making a breastwork cover against possible enemy attack. Walking our horses in single file, we headed for the river, where they would be watered. This done, and after we changed halters, the horse guard took our mounts to graze on the best grass available near our encampment.

Next each man was given a chore: tending the fire; preparing meat; or collecting firewood. It was dark before we ate, collected our horses, changed the light halters, and set stakes around camp at intervals of thirty feet, which would give our animals sufficient grazing space till morning.

Just as soon as we were finished eating, Captain

Weber launched into a discussion about beaver and beaver trapping. "He never stops doing business," Potts whispered, "but he's your kind of man, I reckon. He knows what he knows, and he doesn't waste a lot of words."

"The finest furs are found at the highest elevations," Captain Weber was saying. "Your mature mountain beaver weighs in at between twenty-five and forty pounds. They may not be the biggest beaver, but their fur is the richest and the finest—and brings the best price."

The day had remained clear, and even now, in the evening's final orange glow, the distant peaks of the shining mountains could still be seen.

"Now, when you're trapping lodges, you want to look for the burrow openings. These are found under a fixed object—say, a rock or a log. When a beaver patrols, he uses the water, so you have to know where he uses the ground. Six to eight plews is all you'll get as a rule from a beaver village.

"And don't think your beaver will come to medicine any old where. Learn your beaver trails, study their habits, get to know their patterns." He paused to fill his pipe and look around at the men.

"I'm turning in," Potts said. "I've had enough—how about you?"

"Not just yet. I figure to learn all I can. I've seen a beaver chew off his leg to get out of a trap. That ain't gonna happen to me."

Potts nodded as if he understood, but he slipped away without saying anything. When I turned back to the fire, Captain Weber was lighting his pipe with a burning twig.

.3.

By the time we met up with Smith's brigade near the headwaters of the Powder River, we had made friends with the River Crows and acquired forty-seven horses from them.

After exchanging information and providing Smith's party with several packhorses, we parted company and began trapping beaver as we moved north into the Big Horn Basin. Weber had lectured us on the superior quality of the Crow pelts, and these were the mountain beavers that we were beginning to trap now. As prepared by the Crow women, who were the most skilled Indians in the domestic arts, they brought the best prices in the market.

Major Henry was waiting for us somewhere on the Big Horn River, but we were in no hurry. We wanted to get in all the trapping we could—and the trapping was good.

I guess Potts's luck was due to turn. Just when he'd had a near perfect mend from his accident and we had teamed up again and had our own mounts—well, bad luck just had to come along and knock him down once more. We'd run into an early winter storm while crossing the mountains, and Potts's feet got frozen. His condition was so bad by the time it was noticed that he couldn't dismount without being lifted from his horse.

There was only one way to save Potts, and that was to get him to safety as quickly as possible. The Crow camp on the Wind River, where the others were headed, was our only hope. I volunteered to ride him there, and it was agreed that I would re-join our company on the Big Horn River as soon as Potts was in good hands.

Captain Weber wasn't sure I could find the Crow camp by myself, but several of the men, including Gardner, assured him I would find my way. "He's a born explorer," Gardner said, "and those mates are friends. He'll get him there if he says he will."

We tied Potts to his saddle as securely as we could, and the two of us rode off at a trot. By noon of the following day, we saw the smoke rising from the tepees in the plain below us. A welcoming party of Crows rode out to greet us and escort us into camp. Potts was taken to the lodge of the medicine man and tended to at once.

After spending the night and being assured that my friend was in good hands, I began the long ride back to the Big Horn.

Major Henry had established a fort at the confluence of the Yellowstone and Big Horn rivers, dan-
gerously close to the heart of the Blackfoot country.
Our two parties were separated now by a distance of
more than two hundred miles. As I traveled north, observing the country for beaver and game, my mind
kept returning to the Crow camp, where I had left my
friend, and the company of young trappers led by
Smith. By the time the fort came into view, all I could
think was that it was going to be a long winter, with
little to do and little to learn.

Once I was welcomed into the fort I decided to
speak to Major Henry. My opportunity came when he
called me in to make a report on the Crow village and
Potts's condition.

He poured us each a drink from his flask before
speaking. "Warm your bones," he said as he lifted his
cup. I thanked him as I brought the cup to my lips.

As I studied the major I wanted to tell him what
was on my mind, but he looked so gray and haggard
that I couldn't bring myself to say anything. There
was a long silence before he spoke again. "Weber tells
me that members of the Missouri Fur Company
caught up with Smith in the Black Hills."

"They were led by Gordon," I said, "the one who
helped set the Arikara villages on fire."

A smile began to form on Major Henry's lips, but it

died out before it reached his eyes. "Where are they now?" he asked.

"Wintering with the rest of our men in the Crow village where I took Potts."

"Is he okay?" Henry asked.

I nodded. Major Henry's mind was obviously elsewhere. I waited again for him to speak. "I thought Pilcher would give up," he said, half under his breath.

"Will we trap here come spring, or take the Big Horn down to Crow country?"

"I haven't decided," the major said, and hesitated. He peered over his whiskey cup and looked at me as if he had just remembered who I was. "You're a hard worker, Bridger," he said.

I didn't reply. Instead I brought the cup to my lips and took another sip. We sat like this for a long time. I was aware that the major was slowly slumping in his chair as I watched the sun set through the window behind his back.

It was growing dark in the room when I got up to leave.

.4.

The snows came early, settling in drifts around the fort. We were living on buffalo and the dwindling provisions from Fort Kiowa. The Blackfeet, with whom Major Henry had hoped to trade and barter, were avoiding the fort. There was too little to do, and I was growing more and more restless. I was hoping to devise a plan that would get me back to the Crow village, but I was careful about keeping my thoughts to myself.

One morning, just when I had nearly given up hope, Major Henry called me to his quarters. We hadn't spoken more than a passing word since my talk with him on my return to the fort.

He plunged right in, as if I already knew what was on his mind. "All our trade goods are going to be a burden to us come spring. If we don't get rid of at least some of them before winter ends, we won't be able to begin our spring hunt. We don't want to part with the liquor. . . ." He paused for a moment and looked at me while he unfolded and folded his cupped hands. "It may be the only thing we can entice the Blackfeet with." He paused once more. "But we've got plenty of blankets and gewgaws—things the Crows might trade us peltries for. They've got a talent for preparing hides—"

"Captain Weber gave us a lecture on Crow beaver," I said, trying not to sound anxious.

Major Henry smiled for the first time. "Trouble is, I can only spare a few men, and no packhorses. This isn't the best time to travel, either. Blackfeet'll make meat of anyone they catch traveling their country."

"I know the country, sir."

"I thought of that when the idea came to me. I was trying to think if there would be any volunteers—"

"I'll go, sir."

"You will?" Major Henry said, trying not to sound surprised.

I nodded, and as I did, Major Henry leaned forward and stuck out his hand. We shook on it, which struck me as very peculiar at the time. "I'm sending four men," he said, "and you'll be the chief." He smiled, realizing he had unintentionally used the Indian word for boss.

"You'll travel by snowshoe and dogsled, trading in all the Crow villages as you go. When you reach the Smith party, tell them we'll rendezvous on the Big Horn basin in the spring."

The Crows were expecting us. We had traded our blankets with success along the Big Horn River, and news of our arrival preceded us. Once again I was taken to the chief's lodge. The chief was seated before the fire, crumbling some leaves in a pouch on his lap. "How!" he said, as I seated myself. I returned his salutation and waited.

I felt a rush of cold air as the flap of the tepee opened behind me. I was going to turn when the chief spoke. "Hi-ya, Sorrel Two-Toes."

"How!" Potts answered as he walked toward the fire.

I rose to greet my friend. "How! Sorrel Two-Toes,"
I said, and laughed as we embraced.

"How, Casapy!" Potts replied.

"Casapy?"

"Blanket Chief," Potts said. "That's what the run-
ner who came for me called you. I couldn't imagine
who he was talking about."

"Casapy!" the chief exclaimed, obviously pleased
with my name.

"All right," I said to Potts, "Blanket Chief, but how
did you get the name Sorrel Two-Toes?"

"Sorrel for my hair and two toes for the ones I lost
when my feet froze. The chief here cured me, along
with the medicine man." Potts turned and spoke to
the chief, who motioned for us to be seated.

"Have you learned to speak their language?" I asked
Potts.

"Half sign, half spoken, I'm getting there. The chief
wants us to smoke now, to welcome you as friend and
trader. Tonight there will be a feast, but now you
must rest after your journey." As Potts spoke, the
chief continued to talk with his hands, gesturing toward the mountains and then bringing his hands back
in the form of moving fingers, walking.

"Last evening, late, Smith's party returned from
Union Pass. They had tried to cross the divide but
were stopped by the snow and cold. The chief is
happy for their return. We've been good company for

him this winter. They have much to teach us—and we've got a lot to learn."

The chief was listening intently, but he made no effort to join in our conversation.

"They're the best riders in the world, Jim. As soon as a baby can sit up, they tie it to a saddle, and by the age of four they can ride by themselves. And their women—why, they're the most talented squaws you'll ever meet! They can make anything with their hands. And they like white men. Just make eyes at one of 'em and the next thing you know she'll be crawling in under your buffalo robe."

I was suddenly aware that the chief was holding a long object that had been handed to him in a sheath. We both turned in his direction and waited in silence. Slowly he removed the covering from the long-stemmed pipe that was wrapped with fur and plumed with eagle feathers. He filled the bowl with tobacco from the pouch at his side. Then he lifted it reverently toward the sun, and then down toward the earth, then he pointed it to the north, south, east, and west. As he spoke, his eyes focused on a spot above our heads.

It was my first smoke with an Indian chief—and it reminded me that I was a chief now also, even if only in name. It felt strange, but it also felt right. This wild, strange life somehow seemed more natural to me than the life I had turned my back on only a short time ago.

.5.

We had finished eating and were sitting in a circle around the fire. The Crow chiefs were seated side by side, while Jedediah Smith, Bill Sublette, Jim Clyman, Ed Rose, Tom Fitzpatrick, Potts, and myself completed the circle. These were the men I felt at home with, much more than with the men at the fort. I don't think any of us could have said just why, but what we shared in common was this feeling that there was somewhere to go and something to be accomplished.

Jim Clyman stood up, and after walking toward the entrance of the lodge, he returned with a buffalo robe and a kettle of sand. Placing the robe in front of the chiefs, he carefully turned the robe over, exposing the tanned surface, which he rubbed flat with his hand. Then, reaching into the kettle, he drew out handfuls of sand and began to make land formations.

He first made two mounds, and pointing to them, he looked up at the chiefs. "Tetons?" he asked.

The chief he addressed nodded, using the Indian word, that I had trouble making out.

"Tetons?" Potts whispered at my side.

"The French-Canadian hunters named them," I

said. "I've heard them speak of the Grand Tetons. In their language it means Breasts of the World."

"Those were the mountains we saw then, far to the west," Fitzpatrick said aloud.

Clyman continued to add sand and make new formations, carefully drawing in rivers with a stick. The chief would occasionally rub them out and retrace them with his fingers, all the while speaking in his own tongue.

"He's telling us again that the mountain range we are trying to cross is the backbone of the world," Jedediah said to Potts and me. "The rivers that drain this side of the range all flow to the Atlantic, and the rivers on the other side flow to the Pacific. He says the beaver are so plentiful on the other side that they don't have to be trapped. One has only to walk along the riverbanks and club them with a tomahawk. But he hopes we will change our minds and not go there. He says no white man has ever seen that country."

I felt my face flush with excitement. "No white man!" I exclaimed.

"That's what he says, but we know that a few white men have seen it—Astor and Henry have—but no one knows for sure if there is a pass, or where it is *if* there is one."

"Seedskedee," the chief said now, drawing in a river with his thumb, and then making a motion with his hand to indicate that this river should be our destination.

Clyman pointed to the mountain range that he had begun drawing and which the chief had completed. It stood almost directly between the Crow camp and the Seedskedee River. Jedediah leaned forward, as if imploring the chief to speak.

The chief sat back, his hands in his lap. The crackling fire was the only sound to be heard inside the tent. The chief's eyes rested on Jedediah as he lowered his hand and drew another river running directly into the mountains. "Popo-Agie," he said. And then he backed his finger up to the river's fork and made a line running south to the base of the mountains.

"South Pass," Jedediah whispered, "that must be it."

To my surprise one of the chiefs, whose name was Arapooish, began to speak in our language.

"The Crow country," said he, "is a good country. The Great Spirit has put it exactly in the right place. While you are in it you fare well; whenever you go out of it, whichever way you travel, you fare worse.

"If you go to the south you have to wander over great barren plains; the water is warm and bad, and you meet the fever and ague.

"To the north it is cold; the winters are long and bitter, with no grass. You cannot keep horses there, but must travel with dogs. What is a country without horses?

"On the Columbia they are poor and dirty, paddle about in canoes, and eat fish. Their teeth are worn out; they are always taking fish bones out of their mouths. Fish is poor food.

"To the east, they dwell in villages; they live well, but they drink the muddy water of the Missouri— that is bad. A Crow's dog would not drink such water.

"About the forks of the Missouri is a fine country: good water, good grass, plenty of buffalo. In summer, it is almost as good as the Crow country; but in winter it is cold, the grass is gone, and there is no salt weed for the horses.

"The Crow country is exactly in the right place. It has snowy mountains and sunny plains; all kinds of climates and good things for every season. When the summer heats scorch the prairies, you can draw up under the mountains, where the air is sweet and cool, the grass fresh, and the bright streams come tumbling out of the snowbanks. There you can hunt the elk, the deer, and the antelope, when their skins are fit for dressing; there you will find plenty of white bears and mountain sheep.

"In the autumn, when your horses are fat and strong from the mountain pastures, you can go down into the plains and hunt the buffalo, or trap beaver on the streams. And when winter comes on, you can take shelter in the woody bottoms along the rivers. There you will find buffalo meat for yourselves, and cottonwood bark for your horses, or you may winter in the Wind River valley, where there is salt weed in abundance.

"The Crow country is exactly in the right place. Everything good is to be found here. There is no country like the Crow country."

Chief Arapooish lowered his eyes and looked at us each in turn. "Now we must smoke and bless your journey."

.6.

I awoke the following morning knowing what my next move would be. I was determined to join Smith's brigade and go over the South Pass.

There was a knot in the pit of my stomach as I approached Jedediah. He was cutting cottonwood bark into a neat pile of shavings that formed a mound at his feet. He finished the branch in his hand, and as he leaned forward to pick up another, he looked up at me and said, "We can use a man of your caliber. But what about Major Henry—aren't you the boss of the trading crew? He'll be expecting you to report."

"The crew can carry the message back without me. They'll be leaving in a day or two, as soon as they're rested up."

Jedediah looked at me for a long minute. "Very few men would want to travel over an untried pass in the dead of winter.

"Our horses are worn-out. As soon as they get their

strength back, we'll start. We have ten men now. We can always use one or two more. I want you to understand that we are not free men. I know Henry expects us to join up with him this spring, but there's no time to waste, waiting for the snows to melt—and I can't promise when we'll return. But this doesn't mean we're not working for Ashley. We'll have a good take, if the Crows are right about the region. And if we don't make it—well, it's our skins, isn't it?"

"I'm ready," I said. "I know the odds and I want to go."

"I can use Potts if he's healed," Jedediah said, turning his attention back to his task.

I told Potts the good news as soon as I could find him. He was seated in one of the lodges, near some squaws who were preparing pemmican. "He says he has ten men," I began, "but he says he'll take me on—and you, too—if you're healed up."

Potts frowned. "I wish I were, Jim, but I can't risk it—not in the dead of winter." He was looking at the ground as he spoke, but all at once he lifted his head and smiled. "Didn't I tell you this crew was going to make history? Didn't I? It's all in knowing what you want.

"I almost made it," he continued, "but, well, here I am, too feeble to join up. I have a feeling about this trip . . . Jim, I'm thrilled you're going. I'll see the men take back your report. Don't worry! I'll go myself if I have to."

"Thanks, Dan. I have a good feeling about this trip, too. It'll be a privilege to travel with these men—"

"Well, don't waste any time. You'll be leaving in a few days. You'd better trade for some new clothes. And have some squaw teach you how to use an awl so you can make your own moccasins and shirts when you need them. You want to learn? Well, they've got a lot to teach, and in more ways than one." Potts smiled. "I don't want you to leave here a greenhorn. Did you notice the gray-eyed one over there peeking at us? That was you she was grinning at. You go talk to her now while I look over the horses and see what shape they're in."

.7.

Her name was Whippoorwill. All we could do was talk in signs, but I found out something I never knew before—it's a lot different being alone with a woman than I ever thought it would be. I couldn't tell at first what was happening to me, but even though all we did was sit on our legs and try to talk, I felt different about myself—I mean, *she* made me feel different about myself. I guess I'd have to say that she made me feel like a man, though I don't know how she did it. It was confusing. I felt like reaching over and touching her hand, or maybe even her face, but I was afraid to. I decided I wouldn't tell Potts about any of this because I knew what he had in mind, and I wasn't ready for that just yet. It was so good just to be with Whippoorwill. I don't know if what I was feeling was love, but it was different from anything I had felt before.

Whippoorwill was asking me in sign language if I was going over the mountains. She knew it meant we wouldn't really get to know each other. I could tell she felt sad about it, but what got to me was that she knew I had to go and was somehow encouraging me, supporting my decision. It made me feel good inside.

We were getting so we could read each other's signs pretty well, so when she told me that she—and many others—would also be going over the mountains in the spring, I knew what she meant. Maybe we would meet; maybe, if I looked for her, we would see each other again. I got to laughing when I figured out just what she was saying, and then, without knowing I was going to do it, I reached over and took her hand. She pulled back at first, but before I could withdraw it, she quickly covered my hand with her own.

We sat that way for a long time.

.8.

We were eleven men, riding tall and proud, but I could sense the uneasiness that was in all of us. It seemed to be the thing that connected us and made us a team—explorers who were willing to risk their skins for a glimpse of the great unknown.

We were journeying south, our eyes on the rim of mountains that formed the divide that the Indians called the Backbone of the Nation. It seemed less forbidding now, for we knew that a pass would open for us, an entrance to the other side of the world. I looked from man to man as we rode along. The oldest among us was not much over thirty—Smith, Fitzpatrick, Sublette, Clyman—even Eddie, the only veteran of the group, seemed to be about the same age as the leaders, while the rest of us were even younger.

Shortly after we crossed the Popo-Agie, we came to the base of the mountains, where the bitter, howling winds began to push us eastward into the canyon of the Big Horn River. The men with capotes put up their hoods as we turned and twisted away from the merciless wind that came howling up the gorge, stinging our eyes and taking our breath away. It would rest for a moment but return almost at once, careening in from two and three directions. I held on to the horn of my saddle with one hand while I urged on my packhorse to keep it from falling behind. I had no choice but to let my horse make its own pace, knowing it would follow Smith's mount, that was directly in front, its tail blown horizontal to the ground by the wind that was whistling in our faces.

Through that night and another we continued on, no longer hearing anything but the howling wind. At last we came to the end of the canyon, a journey of thirty miles, though it seemed much longer. A valley stretched before us that led to the river called Sweet-water, which in turn would lead us to the South Pass. This was our hope—our only hope—as we forced our horses on.

But the wind, which we were sure would stop when we left the canyon, grew even worse when we reached the valley floor. We pushed onward to the river against it, as it howled and raged across the valley. At last we came to a clump of willows near the water's edge. We cleared the snow off the lee side of the trees and huddled in pairs under our blankets and robes while we waited for the wind to subside. I closed my eyes but couldn't sleep. I knew that we would be helpless for as long as the storm lasted.

There was still no letup by the second morning, when Clyman and I, wrapping ourselves in buffalo robes, started downriver in search of shelter and food. We trudged along through the heavy snow until we came to a narrow canyon where we found temporary relief by crawling under some rocks. At first I thought it was a mirage when, looking up, I spied a mountain sheep on the opposite cliff. I fired at once, and the sheep fell forward and then rolled down the sheer wall almost at our feet. "C'mon, Clyman," I shouted, and we raced out of our shelter, feeling suddenly alive.

We brought our quarry back to camp at once, but because of the wind, we were unable to make a fire. After several unsuccessful attempts we returned to our blankets to keep from freezing. We looked at each other, too cold and discouraged to speak.

Late that night the wind abated. Clyman was out of his blanket at once, starting a fire, and one by one we joined him, gathering sage and any bits of wood we could find to feed into the flames, after which we began cutting the meat into thin slices for quick cooking. As we ate, we felt ourselves returning to life, our bodies slowly emerging from the cramped hunger and cold of the past days.

"We'll take care of the horses in the morning," Jedediah said. "There may be some buffalo grass to forage on, but I want to cut up some cottonwood bark just the same. They'll need time to get back their strength before we cross the Great Divide."

In the morning Clyman and I traveled down the canyon in search of a permanent campsite, while Jedediah and three others saw to the horses. The rest of the men, under Fitzpatrick's command, formed a hunting party. The buffalo had been driven from the country by the high winds, so we went in search of mountain sheep, which we now knew were both plentiful and unafraid, never having been hunted before.

We found an aspen grove in the valley at the end of

the canyon, where Clyman shot a mountain sheep. After burying it in a snowbank near the stream where we would be camping, we went back for the rest of our party. We ate and rested through the day while our horses browsed and regained some of their strength.

I don't know what would have happened to us if we hadn't been able to rest, because soon after we set out the following morning, we were met by a severe snowstorm. The snow descended in white sheets that threatened to bury us alive. Although we were almost blinded by it, we continued to travel forward, hoping to reach shelter while our horses were still able to move.

At last the snow stopped falling, but it was wet and deep on the ground and slowed our progress. We got down from our horses and gently urged them forward until we reached the campsite Clyman and I had found.

We were now on the valley floor. We had a sufficient supply of water, wood, and game, but the weather would have to change before we could continue on. We made camp and waited. I tried to remember when I had last been warm.

It was two weeks before the sheep recognized danger and disappeared. Although the weather had not improved, we knew we had to push on. Jedediah assured us that the weather would change once we

116

crossed the pass. It was decided that we would cache powder, lead, and some of the other supplies that would not be needed for the spring hunt. We also decided that this would be our rendezvous point should we become separated—and that no matter what happened, we would reassemble here by the first of June.

We took what dried meat we had left and set off once again. It wasn't long before we left the valley and began climbing into high country, in what was to be our final ascent. But soon we were greeted again by howling winds that whipped the snow into a whirling blizzard.

By the end of the second day we had used up all of our dried meat, and the country was barren of game. But the sun shone, warm and promising, and urged us forward. Were we reaching for a new life or were we marching into the jaws of death? Our only water now was melted snow, but because there wasn't even sage to burn, we couldn't melt enough for our horses. We had run out of cottonwood by the sixth day when Clyman and Sublette rode ahead of our party in search of game. They hadn't been gone more than an hour when we heard the single report of a rifle shot. We spurred our horses forward. When we reached our men, they were standing over a buffalo. We rode up and dismounted, and as fast as Clyman could cut meat and throw it to us, we wolfed it down. We hadn't eaten a morsel of food in four days.

Our horses were our only worry now. We had to reach water soon. The Sandy River lay ahead, but how far ahead we did not know. The air was thin and cold, and the snow deepened as we traveled upward, coaxing our weary horses forward. Hour after hour we moved on, our beards growing thick with frost and ice.

I was gradually becoming aware of a vast and endless silence. Before us lay an undulating plain that was like a sea of white waves. In the distance I could make out lofty buttes, like ships, or islands of towers and domes. Others were flat-topped and seemed moored to the horizon. We were on the westward slope of the Great Divide, I was sure of it.

"Look!" Fitzpatrick cried, pointing to the sloping, falling land. We let out a cheer and waved our hats to the horizon, as if we could be seen and heard by the invisible host we felt was witnessing our progress. Jedediah began mumbling a verse under his breath that only he and the wind could hear.

We had crossed the Continental Divide.

.9.

We were traveling downhill into unknown country. The wind continued to blow in gusts, and there was neither shelter for our horses nor wood for a fire to cook our meat and to melt the snow for drinking. The horses were growing weaker and weaker.

By late afternoon our horses were too exhausted to travel. We made a fire of sagebrush and the few buffalo chips we were able to find along the way. Smith, Clyman, and Eddie struck out on foot toward a cottonwood stand in the distance, while the rest of us prepared to cook what meat we had.

It was nearly dark when the men returned with food for the horses. After the horses were fed, we bedded down, but we were up before dawn to resume our journey.

I had lowered my eyes against the glare of the sun reflected by the snow. When I looked up for an instant, I spotted a line of willows in the distance. "The Sandy!" I called out, turning in my saddle.

"You're right!" Fitzpatrick called back, his eyes following the line of trees that were like a dark shadow against the white plain.

Fitzpatrick and I raced our mounts forward, leaving our packhorses for the other men to bring up. We dismounted at the river's bank and ran over its snow-crusted surface, beginning at once to chip away at the ice with our tomahawks. By the time the rest of our party caught up with us, I had hacked out a hole as far down as my arm could reach. "It's frozen clear to the bottom," I shouted, turning to face the others.

"Stand aside!" Clyman ordered, and pulling a pistol from his belt, he aimed into the hole and fired. In an instant water began gushing up in a spray, spreading and freezing over the icy surface. We quickly got down on our hands and knees and began widening the hole to the circumference of our kettles. While some of the men greedily drank their fill, others rushed to the willow bank to water their horses, which were blowing and pawing the ground.

We soon had a blazing fire. Where the sun had melted the snow, patches of grass appeared, faintly green and yellow, providing nourishment for our horses. While they fed and the remaining meat of our buffalo was being cooked, I wandered off downstream looking for game.

There didn't seem to be anywhere for an animal to hide, and for a mile I saw nothing but the occasional track of a rabbit. But suddenly I came upon the tracks of a lone buffalo. I wondered if he had been traveling toward me from the opposite direction and, hearing me, had turned away. Then I remembered that buffalo had poor hearing and weren't alarmed by noises. I also knew that they couldn't see well, either. The tracks were fresh, and he was walking, not running, which meant he hadn't smelled me.

I raced forward as fast as my legs would carry me. The land undulated in a continuing series of rises and falls. I had no warning—in a hollow beyond the slope I had just ascended stood an old bull. He faced me, his tufted tail high in the air as he pawed the ground in rage. Then, to my surprise, he turned, as if he hadn't really seen me, and lowered his head to the ground. I quickly knelt and aimed—barely two hands above the brisket, as I'd been taught—and fired. I heard the smack of the bullet, followed by a puff of dust where the shot had entered. The bull stood motionless for a moment, and then his knees broke and he crashed forward on his nose.

I was still reloading when I heard the men come riding up on their mounts.

"So!" Jedediah exclaimed, "you thought you'd do some scouting on your own."

"It's an old bull," I said, "but meat's meat. Give a hand." I turned and walked down to the animal, trying to keep from smiling. I had killed my first bufler. It hadn't been anything like I'd dreamed it would be, but it was my first, and I had done it alone.

. 10 .

We reached the Seedskedee in two days. We made camp and waited for the river to thaw so we could begin our spring hunt. Dams and dome-shaped lodges were everywhere, as were the felled cottonwoods used by the beaver. All the signs were favorable—the Crows had not exaggerated.

We were surrounded by gray-and-white mountains. The deep blue of the sky seemed to belong to this land. The air was lighter, and the wind, when it blew, felt warm. It was the first sign of spring. Groves of quaking aspens skirted the land that stretched upward toward the mountains.

Deer and elk were plentiful, and there were also geese. We were well fed, and with wood and water aplenty we were content to rest and wait for the hunt to start.

My thoughts often returned to Whippoorwill. At the times when we were closest to defeat, the image of us sitting together would come to me and give me hope. And now, with the weather warming, I thought of her promise to meet me in the spring, and I believed it would come true.

As the melting ice broke loose and began its slow journey to the Pacific Ocean, we gathered together and made our plans. Jedediah would take six men and work the river south, while Fitzpatrick—with Jim Clyman, Thomas Eddie, and myself—would head north. As prearranged, we would meet in June at the river, where we had cached our powder and supplies.

We trapped as we traveled upriver, and every day the weather grew warmer and more welcoming. The beaver were so plentiful that we were often able to shoot them from the bank.

It must have been about the middle of May when

we were visited by three Indians. We were camped on a western tributary far upriver when they arrived. I was alone in camp, it being my turn to skin the animals and dry the hides before binding them into packs.

"How," I said, rising slowly from my work.

"How. How," they announced in turn, moving cautiously forward, and then squatting on their haunches to show that their visit was friendly. I squatted also, facing them, my gun in easy reach, and together we began making signs. They were describing beaver, one of them making the animal's form with his hands, while another slapped the ground, palm downward. I knew that beaver tail was a favored delicacy of some Indian tribes, and I was also aware that beaver was extremely difficult to hunt with bow and arrow.

I was considering what to do when Fitzpatrick walked into camp, followed by Clyman and Eddie. "What are they?" he asked.

"I don't know," I answered, "but I think they'd like some beaver tail to eat."

"Must be Shoshones," Eddie said. He began talking to them in signs. I watched the head Indian make an undulating sign with his hand.

"They're Snakes," Eddie said at once. "Must have come over the mountains, like us. They want beaver, all right. Best give them all they can eat and keep 'em friendly."

From that meeting on we were visited nearly every day by the same three Indians, and always for the same reason. And then one night, in the middle of a snowstorm, they visited us in our sleep and stole our horses.

"Let's go for them," I said, the minute our horses were missed in the morning.

"Which way?" Clyman asked. "They could have gone anywhere. You won't find their tracks in the snow."

"Don't matter," I said. "We can find them. We could split up, go in all four directions—first man sees a track, he can fire his gun."

"I'd be with you, son," Eddie said, "but in this snow—and this being Injun country—we don't stand much of a chance."

"We've come to trap," Fitzpatrick said. "Maybe we'll come on a party of Crows and trade for some mounts, or maybe even another band of Snakes."

"The captain's right," Eddie said. "It won't be the first time I've had to trek out with my beaver packs cached."

I was the youngest, and it wasn't my turn to argue. But I was surprised. Fitzpatrick seemed to me to be as tough as nails, a man who wouldn't back down from a fight. I liked him because he was also an orphan. He'd emigrated by himself from Ireland when he was a boy, which meant he was on his own, just like me. It surprised me that he was backing down.

We continued to trap until early June, adding every day to our store of pelts. But we weren't able to secure new mounts, and fearing we would be late for our rendezvous with Smith, we decided to cache our furs, hang our saddles and other equipment in the trees, and head for the Sweetwater.

We hadn't traveled more than a mile when, turning the point of a ridge, we came face-to-face with five Indians mounted on our horses. Fitzpatrick rushed forward, grabbed hold of the lariat of one of the horses, and ordered the Indians to dismount. We kept our guns trained on them, while Fitzpatrick boldly took possession of our horses.

"That's five of eight," Fitzpatrick said. "We're still missing three horses."

At gunpoint the Indians led us to their camp one mile away. It consisted of six lodges and another eighteen men, plus squaws and children. Among the eighteen men were the Indians we had fed on beaver tails while the ground was still under snow. They hurriedly turned over two of our three remaining horses, but Fitzpatrick was not satisfied. Grabbing one of the Indians, he threatened to kill him if our remaining horse was not returned to us.

We had suspected that it was being hidden in the mountains, and we were right. One of the Indians rushed off and soon returned with our horse. We didn't waste any time getting away, and after retrieving our saddles and furs, we headed for the Sweetwater to meet Smith and the others.

PART FOUR

Discovery

1824

. 1 .

THE FIRST FROSTS OF WINTER CAME, and the mountains changed color daily. They had seemed to me to be the one solid, unchanging feature of the landscape, but they were subject to the same fiery transformation as the rest of the earth. The leaves of the quaking aspens were taking on their autumnal color, and the grasses underfoot turned to crimson and gold. Now I had lived in the valley through all of its seasons.

The summer rains were over, and the sky was again the deep blue that was its special feature. Each sunrise was new and each sunset unique. And every night during the moon's fullness it rode luminous and large over the mountain peaks.

I felt alone, like the moon—and like the moon in its fullness, I felt myself growing as the solitude I was experiencing slowly turned to happiness.

Trapping beaver again, I had time to reflect on my summer with the Crows, from whom I had learned so much about mountain ways and Indian life.

After our rendezvous on the Sweetwater I returned with a few of the men to the valley of the Seedskedee. We were soon joined by others of our company. Johnson Gardner, whose group included Potts, had also come over the South Pass, while Weber's company had crossed over Union Pass. We were all waiting for Ashley's next move. Jedediah was determined to push on to the Columbia, and Fitzpatrick's plans were uncertain. Major Henry had returned to St. Louis in late August, taking a number of men with him, which had reduced our already small company. By late September, word had reached us that Major Henry had given up and turned over the reins to General Ashley, now the sole person responsible for the company. As we waited for his arrival some of the men began talking of becoming free trappers.

But I reasoned that one man could do very little alone. At best he would be free, but how much freer would a man want to be than we were already? To roam these mountains, to trap beaver, and learn the skills of the Indians, and all of this in a land still virgin and more beautiful than my wildest dreams. It was more than enough.

And there was more to this life than just trapping. There was the work we were doing as explorers and adventurers. And although I did not know, as Jedediah did, what my special niche would be in the larger scheme of things, I did know that I wanted one day to carve my own place in it. I had been orphaned, I had learned to be alone, and I could be happy alone, but I did not want to be entirely cut off.

While we waited for Ashley's return I spent the

summer traveling through the valley, sometimes with
Potts, but most of the time alone. I hunted and got to
know the land, and day after day, and often for weeks
at a time, I lived among the Crows, accepting their
hospitality, sharing their food and tepee life. Whippoorwill had not come over the pass with the first
band of Crows, but she had promised Potts that her
family would make the journey before the summer
ended. Potts gave me the message and a good teasing
in the bargain, but I didn't care. I knew now that she
cared for me and that the time was not far off when
wc would see each other again.

The Crows taught me the secrets of tracking, and
the different ways to hunt buffalo and other animals.
They also taught me how to trap and snare small
game, which roots were edible, and how to start a fire
without flint and steel. As important as any of these
things, they taught me their language, as well as the
universal language of signs, with which I could talk to
any tribc of Indians, or any white man who did not
speak my language.

The Crows considered fish an unclean food, but the
Seedskedee was full of trout, which I soon learned to
favor over catfish. I had never fished for trout before,
and I had puzzled for some time over how to catch
these beautiful, speckled fish as they leapt over the
surface of the water, chasing flies and grasshoppers
and bees. One day, wading across the water, I stopped

to watch a bull moose lumber to the water's edge, just out of range. I bent over to have a drink, just as the moose had done, when I saw the dark back of a trout disappearing under a rock beside my foot. Without thinking I reached my hand into the water and lowered it under the trout's belly. When my fingers touched its stomach, it didn't move. I rubbed my fingers along its stomach, and still it remained motionless. I cupped my hand directly under its middle and lifted it out of the water. It didn't squirm or wriggle until I had clamped my other hand over its back. It was over a foot in length and very fat. From that day on I had fish to eat whenever I liked.

I made many friends in the Crow camp, but my closest friend was Broken Arrow, the youngest son of one of the chiefs. He was an expert horseman, as were all of the Crows. It was his job to look after one of the herds belonging to his father, and before long we began caring for the horses together. We spent as many hours as we could riding. Broken Arrow taught me to ride bareback, and also without a bridle—which I needed to know, he said, if I was to become a good horse thief. It would also allow me to keep my balance while shifting to avoid the arrows of my enemy.

I soon learned that Whippoorwill was Broken Arrow's cousin. She had been named Whippoorwill, he told me, because she was born in the season when that bird makes its first call at winter's end.

He knew I was waiting for Whippoorwill, and he assured me that I would be seeing her soon. Finally, in August, she arrived with her family. Whippoorwill was surprised at how quickly I had picked up the language of her people and also the language of signs. Now the two of us had no trouble understanding each other, and the better we knew each other, the closer we became. I don't know whether or not it was out of jealousy, but Broken Arrow wouldn't let us be together alone any more than he could help. And soon we were doing everything together. Whippoorwill was also an excellent rider, and she enjoyed going on hunts with us. She would scrape and cure our deerskins, and once they were ready, she taught me how to use an awl. Together we worked to make me a buckskin jacket with extra long wangs on the sleeves, that I could cut off and use for repairing my clothing. Then she taught me to make my own moccasins: one pair with thick *par flèche* soles for summer, and another for winter made of buffalo hide—thick, soft, and warm.

Whippoorwill also taught me how to make bird calls, and one day she taught me my first Indian song, that we sang as we rode along. It was a happy summer, and a part of me hoped it would never end. But as the evenings grew chill I was reminded that the time was drawing near when I would have to leave her and my new friend, Broken Arrow.

One evening, after I had crawled inside my lodging of bent willows across the river from the Crow camp, I was startled awake by a body touching mine. I knew at once that it was Whippoorwill. She lay down beside me, her warm breath on my neck. It was the first time she had come to me in the night. Her moccasins and legs were cold and wet from having crossed the river. I threw off the blanket covering us and led her to the fire at the entrance of my lodge. A few coals were still aglow. I put on a fresh stick, and removing her moccasins, I placed them against the warm stones surrounding the fire.

It was a warm, still night. We hadn't spoken, but we looked at each other in silent understanding. I rubbed her legs and feet dry with my blanket.

"Why have you come?" I asked.

"Because you are leaving tomorrow. I wanted to say good-bye alone."

"How did you know?"

Whippoorwill did not answer. She looked across the river and then back at me.

"I have to go," I said.

"I understand."

"Something calls me. I do not know what it is."

"When you find what you are looking for, will you return?"

"I will never leave the mountains. They are my home. This vast, unexplored country—I can't say what it is, but I want to know it, I want to live in it as your people do, to be taught and nurtured by the land. And I want to help the land—not just take from it."

Whippoorwill didn't speak. I had never talked to another person in this way. My heart was filled by the mountains, and the words poured out of me as if they had a life of their own.

"I will come next summer. We will ride together again and sing and make the calls the birds make, and we will be happy."

Whippoorwill's moccasins had dried. She placed them on her feet and leaned against my shoulder, her hand resting in the hollow of my arm. I reached another stick into the fire and watched it burst into flame. We crawled back inside my lodge and lay down with our arms around each other and kissed.

The village was asleep. Except for an occasional howl of a dog in answer to a coyote, there was no sound. Only the rippling water and the occasional leaping of a trout for a fly. There was a sweetness in the air that I hadn't noticed before. A full, sentinel moon kept watch until the sun again appeared and Whippoorwill returned to her village.

.2.

We knew that Ashley had set out for the mountains with the intention of reaching us in the spring. Until then we were under the command of Captain Weber, who had assumed leadership upon Major Henry's departure. By the time we reached the northern extreme of Bear River, it was late October. The hunting had been good. We continued to trap through the final days of the season, following the Bear as it wound its way north, then south, again and again, before leading us to a valley where we decided to cache our furs and spend the winter.

Once we had settled in winter quarters, I became more and more curious to know where the Bear River went. We could follow it on foot down to the canyon below our camp, but we could go no farther. The question remained: Where did this unpredictable river go beyond that impassable point? Did it continue south, or did it once again turn north? As we went about the business of making camp—hunting and jerking buffalo meat, erecting winter lodges with cured buffalo skins—the arguments and bets continued. Although I didn't take part in the wagering, I was as interested as anyone to know what became of the river beyond that high-walled gorge. I wanted to see what this mysterious country held in store, for it was not only the river that changed at every bend but the land itself.

One evening, as we sat around the fire waiting for the meat to cook, I muttered, half under my breath, "I aim to find out what lies beyond that gorge."

Johnson was sitting at my side. He turned and looked at me in amazement. "Don't talk foolish!"

"What did he say?" Harris called out.

"Wants to run the river and settle all our bets."

"Too late in the year," Harris replied. "River'll be froze up."

"There's bound to be hostile Injuns," Potts said. "Don't do it, Jim. What difference does it make which way the river turns?"

"It's why it turns that interests me, Dan, and also where it turns. I can't wait till spring. I want to know now. It'll give me something to chew on this winter."

"I wish you wouldn't," Potts said again, "but I know enough not to argue with you once you've made up your mind."

Silence took the place of argument. Everyone looked at me as if I were a touch mad. But once the meat had cooked and we began eating, the wagering started again.

I had helped build the bullboat in which Fitzpatrick had carried our furs downriver after our rendezvous, so I knew how it was done. First I gathered an armful of willows, and after cutting them to the proper length, I fixed them in the ground, setting the butt ends into a four-inch circle. I brought the outer ends together to form a bow, and then I tied them into a rib cage. Next I took twigs of willow and wove them into the ribs, until I had a huge, firm, basketlike structure roughly twelve feet in circumference. I covered the whole frame with buffalo skins, trimming and smoothing as I went along. When I had finished, I built a slow fire to dry the skins. I rubbed buffalo tallow into all of the seams. The tallow, when cooled, would be firm and waterproof. My basket was now a full-fledged boat. All I needed was a long pole to push off with, and after I had gathered everything necessary, including my gun and some dried meat, I was ready to start out.

I began by paddling away, gently drifting with the current. I kept looking back at my companions, who were growing gradually smaller and smaller. I could see the steep cliffs ahead, but the river was broadening and growing more and more luxurious as I traveled along. I heard a clatter overhead and looked up to see a mountain goat. The rock he had loosened echoed as it fell.

The water was growing ever more placid, and the left bank suddenly opened out into a meadow. All at once a cougar appeared, racing along the shore. Then he jumped up to a low ledge where he crouched and waited for me to pass, hanging his head and staring at me, as if he were trying to understand what I was doing there.

Slowly the river changed again. Narrowing as it approached the gorge, its current whirled my boat around so that I had to use my pole. My excitement rose and turned to fear as I was carried faster and faster toward the rock walls that funneled into a *V* and seemed to allow no exit.

The land was my only witness as my boat whirled and shot down the river, gaining speed as we entered the gorge. The rapids ahead turned white. As they drew nearer and nearer it became clear that if the bullboat did not survive, neither would I.

The boat turned and twirled like a top. Sheer cliffs on each side of me seemed to threaten to fall down. I was drenched by the spray as the sky became lost in the water. I clung to the bullboat.

And then it happened. A light shone down, and looking up, I saw the sun—and then the sky. The cliffs fell away to reveal trees and level ground, and looking back at the receding walls of the gorge, I saw that the water before me was a rippling blue.

I had made it! I had come through!

But the boat was leaking. I bailed with cupped hands as I rode into a calm, boulder-filled shallow. The river meandered south for as far as I could see. I was determined to stay afloat for as long as I could, because I knew the boat was beyond repair. At the last minute, with water up to my knees, I guided my craft to the shore as best I could, first with my hands and then with my pole.

I tried to jump to shore, but my boat capsized, sending me sprawling into the icy water. My powder got wet and I nearly lost my gun, but I scrambled ashore and gave a shout of joy. I was alive and safe, and I had survived the craziest and scariest adventure of my life.

After I had built a fire and dried myself and my powder, I decided to walk to a high point of ground in the distance to satisfy myself that the Bear River continued to flow southward, as I was sure by now it did.

The sun was already beginning to sink beyond a distant range of trees when I reached the crest of the hill that held a commanding view of the valley below. I could trace the Bear to its mouth—where a lake stretched out for as far as the eye could see. It was the largest body of water I had ever seen. Was it really a lake? I decided then and there I must see it close, though it appeared to be at least twenty-five miles away.

I made camp and set out in the morning, walking all day toward the large body of water that was now completely out of sight, although, as I drew nearer, I caught glimpses of white water, opaque and still.

I saw no tracks and I heard no sounds as I followed the river that continued its circuitous route on its journey to a lake—if that's what it was.

At last I came to its bank, where I stood, dazed. White water stretched to the horizon. Its motionless surface troubled me, and for some reason the lake seemed even bigger than when I had seen it at a distance. Except for an island or peninsula in the distance, there was nothing else for the eye to behold but white water.

I bent over and cupped a handful of water.

I knew something was wrong the moment it touched my lips. It was brackish.

After spitting out the first mouthful I tried again. Could it really be salt that I was tasting? Yes, by God! It was *salt water!*

.3.

The men looked at me as if they were seeing a ghost. I must have been a sight, with my clothes torn and wrinkled, my hat missing, and my willow pole now a walking stick.

"Here comes old dangersome hisself," Potts hollered out to the others as I trudged into camp.

"We thought you were kilt," Harris said. "We weren't a-looking to see you again, hoss."

I pulled up and leaned on my stick, completely out of breath. "She flows south, boys, but that ain't the half of it. I've discovered the Pacific Ocean!"

"Wait a minute, start at the first," Harris exclaimed.

"It's brackish, I'm saying—and water, far as the eye can see, except for an island away out from land."

"That's Pearl Shell Lake," Harris exclaimed. "That's what the Injuns call it, but no white man's ever set eyes to it till now."

"It's a salt lake, then," I said. "A great salt lake." No one spoke as we stood there in the snow, all of us full of the wonder of something that was beyond our understanding.

What else does this country hold? I thought. What other unbelievable sights are there to be discovered and experienced? I couldn't believe it—I had come looking for beaver and I had found a great salt lake.

I knew now that I would have to search through and explore every region until all of it became as familiar to me as the palm of my own hand.

"Hurrah for the mountains," I called out as I headed for the lodge. It was only then that I remembered that I hadn't eaten a bite of food in nearly three days.

Afterword

Jim Bridger went on to make a lifelong career as a trapper, scout, and guide in the Rocky Mountains.

It wasn't long before he became a partner in the Rocky Mountain Fur Company. Whether in the quest of game or purely in the spirit of adventure, he explored nearly the whole of the region included in the present states of Montana, Idaho, Wyoming, Utah, and the Dakotas.

In addition to his discovery of Great Salt Lake, he was the pioneer discoverer of Yellowstone Park. His customary tales to travelers about the famous geysers and other natural wonders, which were called "Jim Bridger's lies," turned out to be remarkably true, even down to the smallest details. It was said of him that "he could smell his way where he could not see it," and that, "with a buffalo skin and a piece of charcoal," as another explorer put it, "he could map out any portion of this immense region and delineate streams, mountains and the circular valleys called 'holes.'"

With the decline of the fur business and the growth of western emigration, he established Fort Bridger, a way station on the Oregon Trail. To obtain a monopoly of the emigrant business, the Mormons drove him from his holdings, which led Bridger into government service as a scout, a calling he maintained for the rest of his active life.

National forests and towns are named after him, as is Bridger Pass and Bridger Peak. He remains a legend to this day, his name evoking memories of a past impossible to forget.

. GLOSSARY .

voyageurs	Creole boatmen
passe avant	passage each side of the cargo box on a keelboat
beaucoup	very
patroon	boss
par flèche	leather strips

6/87